She knew she shouldn't be doing this, but the temptation was just too strong

Then the impulse hit her. Who would know?

Her stomach trembled as she leaned in and touched her lips to his just once.

Leaning back, she knew it was wrong, but for some reason it felt so right. She leaned in again. This time her kiss was longer. This time it was different. This time he kissed back.

Surprised, she jumped. The penetrating intensity of his dark, sexy eyes sent instant shivers through her body.

"Oh my God, I'm sorry, that was so wrong," she said, moving farther away. He held her in place. "I don't know what came over me, I just—I've never done anything like that before. I don't know what I was thinking, I was—I never lose control like that."

His hand reached out to her, almost in slow motion. His body tensed as his jaw and stomach muscles tightened. He touched her face tenderly and smiled. *"Mia, mi fantasía,* maybe you should lose control more often."

Books by Celeste O. Norfleet

Kimani Romance

Sultry Storm

Kimani Arabesque

Love After All
Following Love
When Love Calls
Pushing Pause

Kimani TRU

Pushing Pause
She Said, She Said
Fast Forward

CELESTE O. NORFLEET

is a native Philadelphian who has always been artistic, but now her creative imagination flows through the computer keys instead of a paintbrush. She is a prolific writer for the Kimani Arabesque and Kimani Romance lines. She also lends her talent to the Kimani TRU young adult series. Celeste lives in Virginia with her husband and two teens.

CELESTE O. NORFLEET

Sultry Storm

KIMANI™
ROMANCE

To Fate & Fortune

 KIMANI PRESS™

ISBN-13: 978-0-373-86117-0

Recycling programs
for this product may
not exist in your area.

SULTRY STORM

www.kimanipress.com

Printed in U.S.A.

Dear Reader,

A lot of you already know that I love writing hot, sensuous romances with great characters and unforgettable story lines. My heroes are handsome and sexy and my heroines are strong and unshakable. In *Sultry Storm* you'll find all that and much, much more. From the very beginning, the story will sweep you up and take you on a whirlwind ride of excitement and passion, setting the stage for the drama that follows. Rescue a stranger, spend the night together and then enjoy a sexual attraction that sets your body on fire…can it get any better than that? The answer is yes.

Mia James faces two storms. Both threaten to break her. As the storm outside lashes out, her guilt at losing her father grows more intense. Stephen, with his own storm, made a promise that he intends to keep. But the promise to watch over Mia didn't prepare him for falling in love with her. As their relationship develops, love grows and the storms, both outside and inside, begin to subside. Together they ride out the sultry storm and find love waiting for them on the other side.

I truly believe that love has a way of healing broken hearts and wounded spirits. Writing *Sultry Storm* was a true pleasure. I'm sure you will find equal enjoyment reading it. If you want to read more about the Morales family and friends, let me know. If you want it, I'll write it. Personally, I'd love to have Natalia's "donor" appear. Make sure to check out my other hotter-than-hot romances.

You can contact me at conorfleet@aol.com or P.O. Box 7346, Woodbridge, Virginia 22195-7346.

Don't forget to check out my Web site at www.celesteonorfleet.com.

Enjoy!

Celeste O. Norfleet

To Brenda Jackson and Carmen Green.
It was a pleasure writing with you ladies.

To Kelli Martin—-thanks for the inspiration.

Chapter 1

"The U.S. National Weather Service has issued an updated severe weather warning. Tropical Storm Ana has upgraded to a Category One hurricane and is headed northeast at approximately fifteen miles per hour. Local authorities are warning…"

"Whoa." The car rocked from side to side as the winds raged, taking turns beating against both sides. Mia James gripped the steering wheel tighter and held steady against the near eighty-mile-per-hour winds. She took a deep breath and released it slowly, trying to calm her fraying nerves.

Driving on the vast expanse of Florida's scenic Overseas Highway was usually a pleasurable experience. Divided by the emerald waters of the Atlantic Ocean on one side and the Gulf of Mexico on the other, the view was breathtaking. But not today. Today the waters were gray, the sky was gray and the horizon looked ominous.

Mia knew it was guilt that was pushing her to do this, but that didn't matter now. What mattered was that she was finally doing it. It was long overdue and her obligation was clear. She needed to make things right the only way she could.

Her dad was right. He was always right and yet she hadn't listened to him. If she had, none of this would have happened. Her heart wouldn't have been broken and he'd still have his honor and his legacy. But she didn't, and now she needed to put it right.

"With the eye less than seventy miles offshore, landfall is expected directly across the Florida Keys in about..."

"Okay, that's enough doom and gloom from you, radio announcer," Mia said impatiently, then pressed the button on the steering wheel to tune to another station. "Let's see what else is going on."

"The storm has maximum sustained winds predicted near ninety miles per hour and with the probability of higher gusts. We're in for a major storm system today. If you're not prepared I suggest..."

"Don't care. Next," she said, pressing the button again. She glanced at the empty lane beside her and noticed that the train of brake lights and bumper-to-bumper traffic had long since dissipated. There were only a few cars on the road, and all of them were headed north.

"The weather is definitely getting worse..."

"No joke, next," she muttered sarcastically as she turned to the next station.

"The storm is expected to reach the area within the next five hours."

"Looks to me like it's already here, dude. You're late," she muttered, and then pressed another button, then another. Frustrated, she turned to several more stations. She'd been listening to the same rhetoric off and on for the last few hours. At this point she was tired of it. Every station spouted the same severe warnings, and she didn't need a radio announcer to tell her that she was headed into trouble.

The idea of driving directly into the path of a Category One hurricane was ludicrous. But at this point she was driving on pure adrenaline. She didn't have much choice. Her deadline was today, and getting away from it all was exactly what she needed to do.

She pressed through a few more buttons until she found something of interest. Smooth jazz played in the background, plus the DJ had a soothing voice—exactly what she needed. "Perfect."

"All right, folks, listen up, it's no joke out there. Hurricane Ana is picking up momentum. The Keys are getting hit hard with heavy rain and wind gusts. Authorities are warning to expect the worst. If you're out in this, you need to get indoors fast. It ain't pretty and it's not for the faint at heart. So do whatever you need to do to be safe."

Mia looked out the front windshield. He was definitely right, it wasn't pretty out here. The rain came down so hard she could barely see the highway through the rapid-fire windshield wipers. Thankfully this was just about over. She abandoned the highway at the next exit. Finally she was in Key West. She breathed easier for the first time in over an hour.

"For those on the road helping others, I'm tippin' my hat, thanks. We appreciate your time, devotion and dedi-

cation. On a personal note, I'd like to give a special shout-out to my homeboys, Stephen Morales and Lucas McCoy. I know you guys are helping others out there, so take care and be safe.

"One more thing. I got a message from my good buddy Deputy Sheriff Morales asking me to pass on a good word of advice. Stay in your homes and off the roads unless absolutely necessary. And I gotta add a piece to that. The streets are dangerous right now, so be safe and listen to him. He's out there doing his job. Help him out and do yours. Stay inside.

"Okay now, here's another updated weather advisory. Hurricane Ana is still hovering less than a hundred miles south of Key West. Wind gusts range seventy-five to ninety miles an hour locally. Expect fallen debris and dangerous travel, so stay inside. Sit tight and let her pass."

"Unfortunately, not an option," Mia muttered, coming to a complete stop and looking at the horrendous sight. The traffic signal had fallen down and the street was littered with just about everything. She looked both ways, then proceeded across. The heavy winds shook the car again, but she held tight. The storm was definitely getting worse. The rain was horizontal and the winds were brutal.

"I have a few local warnings. The Seven Mile Bridge is looking bad. It'll probably close to all non-emergency traffic…"

When another strong gust of wind hit the car, Mia grasped the steering wheel tighter. This was even worse than being on the bridge. Her nerves were rattled and her hands shook. She needed to calm down.

"If you're headed out toward Tingler Island, local

authorities are warning everyone to turn around. Bottom line, folks, sit tight and I'll get you through. This is Terrence Jeffries, the Holy Terror, easing your evening. Sit back, be calm, relax and listen."

Soft melodious jazz began playing. "Okay, this is more like it. Exactly what I need." Mia smiled and nodded her head to the easy rhythms. "Thanks, Holy Terror," she said, hoping to feel more at ease. She turned the volume up higher.

Holy Terror. She'd heard of him, of course. Everybody knew the Holy Terror, Terrence Jeffries. On the football field he was legendary, and his so-called antics in romance were almost as well-known. Mia had watched him play football when her father was alive. He was awesome.

"So, you're a radio disc jockey now, cool." She tried to do as he instructed and relax, but it was getting more and more difficult to see and drive. At one point she realized she had gone in circles. It was no use. She was miserably lost. Each turn was the wrong turn, and the horribly flooded roads didn't help. She reached over and adjusted her pre-programmed GPS. The monotone voice announced new directions to the courthouse.

She hadn't been to Key West or her father's house in almost three years and everything about the town seemed different. Following instructions, she turned onto a familiar street that led directly to the center of town. But the street was blocked by a huge uprooted tree. She pressed the button on the GPS for an alternate route, backed up and continued.

She zigzagged through scattered debris down the next few blocks. At one point she quickly glanced down at the clock. It was three minutes to five and according to the

GPS, she was still a few miles away. That was when she heard the loud crash. Looking up, she saw the better part of a tree had just fallen across the road. She slammed on the brakes and hydroplaned before coming to a complete stop. Her heart racing, her breathing fast and furious, she stared at the tree that narrowly missed her.

"Are you kidding me?" she screamed, slamming her palm on the steering wheel in frustration. She hit the wheel again and again, then began breathing even harder. "No, no, I will not hyperventilate, I will not feel sorry for myself and I will not let this get to me," she said, trying to calm herself down.

"Okay, enough of this pity party. I can do this. I will do this," Mia affirmed with determination. After a few minutes she gathered her nerve, then glanced at the clock on the dashboard. It was five o'clock already. She backed up and quickly sped around the tree. To her surprise she met two headlights with flashing red and blue lights coming directly at her.

Reacting fast, she steered out of the way, giving the speeding oncoming police jeep just enough space to wedge between her and the fallen tree. As soon as they passed each other, they came to a complete stop. In the rearview mirror. Mia saw the officer open the car door.

"Oh crap, this is all I need," she muttered as she watched him run to her car. Frustrated, she muted the music and reached for her pocketbook to get her license and registration. As soon as he got there she opened the window, and heavy rain poured in. She began digging through her purse for her ID.

As the driving rain poured down his face, the officer hunched toward her window and squinted down at her. "Lady, are you out of your mind, driving reckless in a hurricane?" he asked. His voice boomed as loud and thunderous as the rumbling above them. Irritated and infuriated, he stood firm against the whipping wind gusts beating down on him.

"Me? What about you? You were driving like a madman around the tree. You could have killed us," she said, equally infuriated while still digging for her ID.

"What?" he yelled as a loud clap of thunder sounded right above them. "I'm a deputy sheriff on an emergency call. What exactly are you doing out here?"

"What?" she yelled and continued looking for her license and registration.

He leaned in closer, bowing the brim of his hat against the wind. "All nonessential personnel are ordered off the streets. You need to be inside now," he yelled over a loud roll of thunder as wind-driven rain peppered his face harder.

Finding her ID, she finally looked up. The first thing she saw was smooth caramel skin, dark eyes and a too sexy mouth. Like her, he was wet, soaked. Her breath caught in her throat. She half smiled, as chapter three, page thirty-seven of her book quickly popped into mind, *Getting Wet for Two*. Feeling herself flush, she covered her face and shook her head. Good Lord, between that book and the sexually repressed thing, she was becoming obsessed with men and sex. But that wasn't the point right now.

"Ma'am, hey, are you all right?" the officer asked, softening his tone with concern after seeing that she was obviously distraught by their near collision.

She nodded and quickly looked away. "Yeah, I'm fine, just a little rattled."

"You shouldn't be out here."

"Look, I'm sorry. I didn't see you coming around the tree."

"I had my siren on," he said sternly.

"With the thunder and wind, I didn't hear it," Mia said.

"Ma'am, you realize you're driving down a one-way street? You could have been killed, or killed someone driving that fast around an obstruction."

"Sorry, I didn't realize it was one way and I didn't realize anyone was coming." She glanced up quickly, looking down the street then finally up at him. She lowered the brim of the baseball cap she wore and covered her face with her hand as she blinked away the rain pouring down. "All the other streets are blocked and this is the only other street I knew to get me into town. The tree just fell in front of me."

"As I said, the roads are all closed except for emergency personnel. You need to get off the streets. A mandatory evacuation had been issued. I'll be happy to escort you back to the highway or to the nearest shelter."

"What if I don't want to be evacuated or go to a shelter?"

"That's not an option. All tourists must be evacuated."

"But I'm not a tourist. I was born here and I lived here. I'm just trying to get home," she insisted.

"You have Georgia plates, ma'am. That makes you out of state."

"I borrowed the car," she lied quickly.

"Ma'am…" Obviously he did not believe her.

"Okay fine, it is my car, but I'm just trying to get to an appointment in town and I'm already late."

"The town's businesses are all closed."

"No, they're expecting me."

"I'm sorry, ma'am, visitors and tourists are being ordered to evacuate now. If you keep straight and go down to the next intersection and make a right, you'll see the entrance ramp to U.S. 1 north. It'll take you back to the mainland. The bridge will be closing shortly. You'll have just enough time to clear the area." He nodded. "Thank you, please drive carefully." He turned and hurried back to his jeep.

She sat for a moment, thinking that he was right. This was insane. "Why am I doing this?" she asked, nearly in tears.

The question didn't linger long. She knew exactly why she was doing this. Still, she couldn't help thinking that just twenty-four hours earlier another school term had ended and she was packing to separate herself from the personal drama that had been unfolding. Paradise Island had been her destination. White sand beaches, crystal-blue water and not a cheating, backstabbing man in sight.

But that was before the call came, alerting her to the situation. The Monroe County courthouse clerk was formal and detached when she stated the facts. Since Mia had failed to pay the taxes and mortgage owed on the property, the house was going into foreclosure. All attempts to contact her had gone unanswered, so the county had no alternative. The bank was going to sell the house and land, recoup the debt payments, then forward her whatever was left.

Mia was still too stunned to believe it. Her father's home, the only thing she had left of him, was about to be auctioned off without a second thought. Her ex-fiancé had evidently decided not to tell her about the foreclosure, and by the time she'd found out it was almost too late. Now her plan was simple, to drive to the county clerk's office in town, fill out whatever papers she needed to fill out, and then get to her father's house and ride the storm out there.

But truth be told, she needed to get away. She couldn't stand being in Atlanta another minute. Knowing that her ex-fiancé and his new coed wife were coming back to town only prompted a quicker retreat from the city. Of course, driving into the storm wasn't a great idea, but it did give her a valid reason to leave.

She wondered what she saw in Neal in the first place. For three years she'd wasted her time and money on a man who wouldn't know class if it jumped up and bit him on the rear. Her father had been right all along.

In the rearview mirror she saw the jeep, its flashing lights turned off. Now he was exactly what she needed to put her nonrepression to the test. He was tall, maybe a little over six feet, nicely built, probably just over thirty years old, sexy and attractive. "Yep, he'd be perfect." She laughed nervously. "Okay, but right now, girl, you needed to focus," she told herself. She pressed the Mute button, filling the car with music again. Nodding her head, she reached over to her GPS and found a new route into town.

Chapter 2

Deputy Sheriff Stephen Morales picked up the fallen radio in his jeep and pressed the Return button.

"You still there?" he asked, breathing hard from the excitement.

"Yeah, I'm still here. What happened? Do you need me to send help your way?" Terrence asked. "I was just about to call into police dispatch."

"No, I'm fine," he said as he looked up in the rearview mirror to see the red taillights continue down the street. "Do me a favor and reiterate that part about staying off the roads. Apparently your listening audience didn't hear it the first few dozen times you mentioned it."

"What happened?"

"It's what didn't happen. A head-on collision."

"Come again?"

"I just had a near miss with some crazy lady speeding to get to an appointment in town."

"But everything in town is closed."

"Yeah, I tried to tell her that. Listen, I better check in and see about the bridge situation."

"All right, be safe out there. If you need anything else call me. I'll be on the air for the duration. Do you need anything now?"

Stephen didn't respond; he was staring up at the rearview mirror. His thoughts spun wildly back to the driver in the car. He didn't get a good look at her face, but there was something… "It couldn't be her," he muttered to himself.

"Couldn't be what? Hey, you sure you're okay out there? I can send someone to you," Terrence said. Stephen still didn't respond. "Stephen, you there?" Terrence called out, his voice getting louder.

Hearing his name, Stephen blinked back. "Yeah, yeah, I'm just checking something out, that's all. I thought I saw something. I'm not sure."

"Man, you just got out of the hospital a few days ago. You need to take it easy out there. This isn't the kind of weather you need to play with."

"No, I hear you. I'm fine. So how are you and Warrick's niece doing?"

"You wouldn't believe me if I told you."

"Sounds serious," Stephen said, surprised by Terrence's near obsession with the woman.

"Serious was two minutes after I met her."

"In that case it sounds like the Holy Terror has finally been tamed. I wish you and Sherrie the best. Let me know when to get my tux pressed."

"Will do. Be safe," Terrence said.

"Back at ya," Stephen said, and then signed off.

"Mi fantasía," he muttered. It was his imagination,

of course. Too many hours on duty, too many coffees, too little sleep, plus coming off the incident last week, he was understandably exhausted. There was no way he saw what he thought he saw.

Of course, he'd only really seen her once, at the funeral, nine months ago. She seemed small and delicate at the time. She leaned on the man with her, and Stephen was so filled with jealousy that he walked away and never looked back. He regretted not staying and at least introducing himself.

Stephen glanced up, seeing a set of red taillights pass down the street. He was sure it wasn't her. He pressed the Call button on his walkie-talkie. "This is Morales checking in, over," he said.

The response was instant. "Hey, everything okay out there?"

"Natalia, is that you? What are you doing at dispatch?"

"Sheriff has me sitting here playing nursemaid."

"You're pregnant. What do you expect?"

"Equal consideration," she said, frustrated.

"I wouldn't mind a little equal consideration right now. I'm soaking wet out here."

"That's why you stay in the jeep."

"Easy for you to say. You're nice and cozy inside."

"Yeah, yeah, you just be careful out there. Remember, you're not at one hundred percent just yet. As a matter of fact, you're lucky you're even out there. You're still listed as injured."

"I'm fine, don't worry about me, I think I've done this hurricane thing once or twice."

"Every hurricane is different, you know that. So don't get too cocky out there, unless of course you want me to come out there and rescue you again."

He laughed at the memory, but she didn't join in.

A few weeks ago Stephen had been doing backup for Natalia as she rescued drunken tourists who'd crashed their car down a ravine. He'd saved Natalia and the tourists, but then found himself in trouble, needing Natalia to save him. He was injured in the process, and afterward she was put on desk duty by the sheriff, due to her advancing pregnancy.

"Yeah, you laugh now, but wait until you're stuck on desk duty for the next three weeks," she said, prompting Stephen to laugh even harder. "All right, back to business. What was the call?"

"It was just a tourist driving down Waterway Street in the wrong direction. We almost ran into each other."

"Jeez, not another reckless tourist," she said with obvious annoyance. "They must think this is some kind of game. When will these people learn that hurricanes are no joke?"

"That's a fact," Stephen said, glancing in the rear-view mirror. "Oh, there's another tree down on Waterway Street and a utility pole on Main."

"Roger that. With the winds getting stronger, we can expect a lot more downed trees and poles. We're up to eighty-five miles per hour on the bridge, and this hurricane is still hours away."

"It's gonna be a bad one."

"Okay, listen up, the bridge is about to close, but we still have a few stragglers. They're being directed to the local shelters."

"Got it," Stephen noted as he glanced in the rearview mirror. But the car had long since turned out of sight. "I'll head over to the bridge now."

"Negative. Take a pass. We've got the bridge

covered. Remember, you're not technically on active duty yet. Anyway, both northbound and southbound traffic are closing so we shouldn't see anyone this way. At this point anyone in the Keys now is staying here until the hurricane passes."

"Affirmative," Stephen said. "I'm gonna swing by the shelters and check them out."

"Roger that. Afterward, why don't you knock off? Everything's covered and you've already done a triple shift."

"I might just do that," Stephen said.

"The band has been giving us some trouble, so stay up on the local channel for more details. We're also passing info through Terrence. He's going to be on air for a while."

"Got it."

"All right, be careful. Talk to you later, out."

"Roger that, out," Stephen said, and then placed the radio on the seat beside him. The familiar tension in his neck and shoulders strained his muscles. He rubbed the soreness and gently touched his upper arm. The stitches were gone, but the nagging pain was still there. It was his second day back, much earlier than required, but every officer was asked to help with the evacuations. He looked up at the dark sky. This was definitely going to be a bad one.

Having lived in the Keys all his life, Stephen knew these storms all too well. What was once paradise could quickly turn into a living hell. Advance planning and keeping a cool head were the keys to survival. Unfortunately few adhered to the simple precautions. He'd been in too many storms not to know the trouble when he saw it coming. Slow and deliberate, Hurricane Ana had all the makings of trouble.

Stephen looked up and stared in the rearview mirror. The familiarity of the driver still stayed with him. He knew it couldn't be. He ran through the meeting quickly. The baseball cap was pulled down too low for him to see her face clearly, still, she looked so much like the woman in his dreams. But he was certain she couldn't be. She hadn't been here in the last nine months since the funeral or even the three years before. There was no reason for her to come down here now. Besides, no one in their right mind would venture into a hurricane. In his exhaustion he must be imagining things.

As if to make a point to himself, he yawned. He'd been on evacuation duty for the last twenty-four hours. He always mused at the absurdity of convincing someone to leave the area for their own safety. But it was his job to convince them, even conjure or beg, if necessary. So, with one last glance in the mirror he shifted gears and steered the jeep to the nearest shelter.

A few miles down the road Mia's cell phone beeped. She pressed the button on the steering wheel to mute the radio, and then activated the car's phone speaker system. "Hello."

"Where are you now?" Janelle asked.

"Are you there yet?" Nya added.

Mia signed heavily. It was Nya Kent and Dr. Janelle Truman on conference call again. They'd been calling her off and on for the last few hundred miles. She loved and adored them and usually delighted in hearing from them, but today they were driving her crazy. Both were her stepsisters, as both their fathers had been married to her mother at one point. Each of the marriages eventually failed, but the three stepsisters remained best friends. "No, not yet, but I'm close. I'm off the bridge and in town," Mia said.

"It's about time. You left Atlanta over ten hours ago," Nya said. "Shouldn't you be at the courthouse by now?"

Before Mia could answer, Janelle said, "What makes you think the county office will still be open when you get there? They'll probably be closed if the hurricane is as bad as the newscasters say."

"They'll be open. They have to be," Mia said woefully.

"What you have to do is turn around and come back here."

Here we go again, Mia moaned inwardly. It was the same conversation all over again and she wasn't in the mood to hear it. When she first told them her plans to drive down to the Keys while under a hurricane watch, they were determined to talk her out of it, citing Hurricane Katrina as their main argument. She was finally able to convince them of the unpredictability of forecasting hurricanes and the extreme unlikelihood of the then tropical depression upgrading to hurricane level or even coming close to the Keys. Eventually they relented. "You guys are starting to sound like nagging six-year-olds in the backseat."

"At the very least you should have flown," Janelle said.

"As I said the last three times you told me that, Janelle, flights headed in this direction were being diverted."

"What about a private plane?" Janelle asked.

"*All* flights were being diverted," Mia repeated.

"Actually, not all flights," Nya interjected. "I have a friend who can fly you just about anywhere at any time. All I have to do is—"

"Not now, Nya," Mia said, getting slightly exasperated by her sister's persistence. But to her credit, Nya probably did know someone who could fly in this madness. She had a network of associates who could do just about anything at any time. Her connections, thanks to her father, both legal and not so legal, were mind-boggling. "Guys, like I said before, it takes at least twelve hours to get here ordinarily. But with the storm, driving is slow, even if the roads into Key West are practically empty."

"Empty? Well hell, of course they're empty. Everybody with some sense has evacuated. I still can't believe you're driving down there in the middle of a hurricane. It's insane," Nya said.

"Don't worry so much, the hurricane is something like seventy-five miles away. It's raining and a little windy, but it's not that bad," she blatantly lied, "and besides, you know I didn't have much choice."

"You could have waited or gotten someone else to do it for you," Janelle said.

"If you'll remember, that's what got me into this mess."

"Stop blaming yourself, Mia. This isn't your fault, no one knew this was going to happen."

"My dad knew." At Mia's reply, her friends' protests went silent. "I had to come today," she said after a while. "The clerk told me that the house is going into foreclosure and an auction is imminent. I can't let that happen. I need to be there before the place closes at five so I can file the extension papers."

"But, Mia, are you hearing the weather reports? They say that this hurricane is a Category One now," Janelle said.

"And it's heading directly for the Keys," Nya added.

"Yeah, I know, I heard," Mia said, "but I have plenty of time to get to the county office, file my petition and get out of here before it hits."

"Okay, wait, listen to this," Nya interrupted. "With no signs of weakening, Hurricane Ana is strengthening—"

Mia cut her off. "You don't have to read every weather report you find to convince me that it's going to get bad. I know it will."

"Apparently I do, because apparently you don't." Nya groaned. "You know she's running away," she said plainly.

"I know she is," Janelle agreed.

"It's all because of that stupid, childish, self-centered, egotistical fool," Nya added.

"Ah, yes, Neal, her so-called fiancé," Janelle clarified.

"Do you two mind not talking about me like I'm not here?"

"I still can't believe he posted that e-mail like that. What a jerk."

"He's a jerk all right, just like I said before."

This was one conversation Mia had no intention of hearing. "As usual, guys, talking about the drama in my personal life has been a blast for me, but according to the GPS, I'm almost there. I need to concentrate. I'll call you back after I take care of everything."

"What about your trip to Paradise Island?" Nya asked.

"I'm packed and headed there after I leave the Keys. Assuming the weather cooperates," she added.

"All right," Janelle said, "drive carefully."

"Yeah, and don't forget to call us," Nya added.

"I won't forget. Talk to you guys later," Mia said, and then pressed a button on the steering wheel to disconnect the conference call.

The car went silent except for the howling winds and pouring rain. Oddly enough, they were a welcome relief after Nya and Janelle. She knew they were right. She was running away. But what else could she do? Her fiancé of three years had dumped her and eloped to Vegas and there was no way she was going to be there when he and his wife got back. She was already humiliated enough.

The e-mail that ended their relationship was made public via the "Reply All" feature. She still had no idea how it happened. But there it was on the campus gossip Internet site for all to see. Professor Mia James Dumped by Professor Neal Bowes.

He had called her cold, unfeeling and sexually repressed. *Sexually repressed.* The two words were now forever attached to her name in cyberspace. It still infuriated her. She was not repressed. She might be a bit controlling and slightly restrained, but she was definitely not sexually repressed.

She glanced at one of the books she'd been reading and smiled. She was definitely not repressed and she intended to prove it to herself as soon as she got to Paradise Island.

"Nya is right. Neal was a stupid, self-centered, egotistical jerk."

Chapter 3

Finally, Mia found the office building. She parked, tugged her baseball cap lower and then got out. In torrential rain she ran through massive puddles to the door and pulled it open. It didn't budge. She tried again; still nothing. Wearily, she stepped back and stared up at the brick building hoping to see some semblance of life, the windows were boarded. "No, no, no," she repeated. "Please don't be closed." She shut her eyes and said a silent prayer. Then she tried again, and that was when she saw the note on the door stating that the office would be closed due to current weather conditions.

Standing there, soaked, her tears mingling with the rain, she just stared at the sign on the door. It was over. She'd lost her father's home.

Frustrated rage welled up inside of her. She should have listened to her father. None of this would have happened. She should have taken care of this herself. She should have dumped Neal years ago. But the should haves were a moot point. It was too late. Now there was nothing left to do but go to the house and collect whatever memories she could.

She ran back to the car and got in. Soaked to the bone, she turned on the ignition and with the wipers on the highest setting, she steered the car away from the flooding curb. It was time to move on.

The streetlights were out and she hadn't seen another car on the road since she drove into town, except the cop's jeep, of course. She turned the corner in the direction of her father's house. Instantly it felt like she was driving in a wind tunnel as blustering winds rushed her from all directions. At least she was off the main highway and away from police cars.

With that thought, she began thinking of the officer who had stopped her earlier. His expression had been curious. When she looked up at him his eyes had seemed to widen in surprise. If she didn't know any better, she would have said that he knew her. He did look somehow familiar… But that was impossible. She didn't really know anybody here anymore.

A heavy wind shook the car and brought her back to her current reality. The storm was definitely getting worse. There were fallen branches and windblown debris everywhere. Buildings were haphazardly boarded, with the eerie howling winds and horizontal rain, the area looked like a ghost town.

A strong wind pushed the car into a gutter-side puddle. She lost control and felt the car hydroplaning in water much deeper than she anticipated. Mia grasped the steering wheel and held tight. She allowed the car to come to an almost stop before braking then reaffirming control. She needed to focus on getting to her father's house now.

But her nervousness intensified as she drove through town. Near panic, she felt as if a noose had been tied around her throat. The puddles were too deep, the rain too steady and the wind was ferocious. Having at times stayed with her mother in Boston, she was adept at driving in all kinds of weather, but this was insane. Then, moments later, she was off the main road and headed to the small area she knew like the back of her hand. She hadn't been here in years, but thankfully it was still the same. She turned the radio on and scrolled through static until she found Terrence Jeffries again. "Okay, Holy Terror, get me out of this mess." Jazz played as she drove through a darkened intersection of the now ghost town.

"I can do this, I can do this," she muttered to herself, as the storm bore down around her and the winds, howling like a wounded creature, jostled the car again. At five-thirty it looked as if it was midnight. The dark gray sky had turned vicious. She gripped the steering wheel tighter, feeling the wind whip up again.

Few things unsettled Mia. That's how her grandmother had raised her. *Never lose your cool. Never show your anger. Never lose control.* She reached back, remembering her grandmother's words. *Always, always, be in control.* As she repeated the mantra and continued driving, till she suddenly saw flashing lights in the rearview mirror. "Crap."

Rain spotted her face as soon as she rolled the window down. "Not again," she breathed out exasperatedly, as she waited for the police officer to get to her car. The last thing she needed was an overzealous cop hassling her. "Yes, Officer," she yelled over the wind's roar as soon as he arrived. "What did I do this time? Break the speed limit, forget to put on my turn signal, not pause long enough at a yield?"

As soon as he saw her face, he knew it was her. But this wasn't the place or the time to talk. He needed to get her off the road and out of this weather. "No, ma'am," he said as calmly as possible. "I'm sorry, but for your safety, you're gonna need to turn around and get to a shelter. I'll escort you. Please turn and follow me."

"But I'm almost there. I'm going to my father's house and it's just a few miles up the road. Once I get there I swear I'll stay put until this is over. Just let me get to his place, okay?"

"Most residents have evacuated for their safety," he said.

"Believe me, he's still in the area," she assured him. "If you're concerned for my welfare then follow me to my dad's house to make sure I get there safely."

"Please follow me, ma'am."

It was like he didn't hear a word she said. "That's not gonna happen, Officer. As I said before, I'm fine. So you can go play superhero and save somebody else," she said, pressing the button to roll the window up again. She turned to face front and shifted gears to Drive, but stopped when she heard the tapping. She rolled the window down again. "Yes?"

"I'm afraid I'm going to have to insist you follow me this time, ma'am."

"Like I just said, that's not gonna happen," she defied.

"I think it will," he affirmed, challenging her defiance.

She looked at him squarely. He returned her stare. It was just her luck to be stopped by a gorgeous cop with superhero issues. Apparently reasoning with him wasn't going to work. "Look, alienating the local authority isn't my intent, so don't take this personally, but I'm not going to any shelter, now or ever."

Stephen smirked. Stubborn and determined, she was so much like Leo it was amazing. "You will follow me to a shelter," he said, just as determined.

"I'll tell you what, you can consider yourself off the hook. If I kill myself out here, then it's on me. So just let me go on my way." The officer didn't respond. He just stood there stoic. "We can argue this until the skies clear, but…"

"I'm sorry, ma'am, please follow me now," he said firmly, then without waiting for her reply, turned and hurried back to his jeep.

"Not now. Not today of all days," Stephen muttered, as he shook his head and headed back to the patrol jeep. "What is she doing here in the middle of a hurricane?" He had expected her to come eventually, but not in this.

This was all wrong. It was not how it was supposed to happen. He was going to get her down here, talk to her and then resolve his feelings one way or another. He needed her out of his system. This fantasized lovesick infatuation was disrupting his judgment and interfering with his life. He hoped that seeing her and talking to her would terminate his obsession. He needed to resolve his feelings for her, but right now he needed to get her to safety.

Mia rolled her window up and just sat there. She watched the rain continue pouring and the wipers splash back and forth. She'd spent over a dozen hours driving into a hurricane, only to find the county office closed, and now this. She was so close. Suddenly a barrage of thoughts came at her. She was always so close, but never quite there. She'd been so close to getting the position as department head, so close to getting married, so close to being happy, so close to fulfilling her dreams. But close just wasn't good enough anymore.

The officer flashed his lights, then made a U-turn, expecting her to follow. She pulled out and drove down the road, not turning around. She glanced up, seeing him make another U-turn to follow her. "Sorry, Officer, I'm in control," she said belligerently. "Fine, you can follow me all the way to my father's house."

In the rearview mirror she saw his jeep come closer. Then in an instant it vanished as part of a tree crashed behind her. She saw the jeep swerve then disappear off the road.

The crash was unmistakable. Whether her superhero cop survived was anybody's call.

Chapter 4

"Oh my God, what have I done?" Mia jumped out of her car in a panic and ran to the side of the accident. She looked down the steep ridge in horror. The guardrail was completely sheared as the jeep had apparently slid down an embankment and was wedged against what was left of two fallen trees. It was smashed, dented and completely snarled by the impact. "Oh God, please don't let him be dead, please don't let him be dead," she muttered a prayer as she searched for a path to get down to the wreck. "Officer, Officer, hello, can you hear me?" she yelled down at what was left of the police jeep. There was no answer.

"I killed him," she muttered, feeling the tears of sorrowful guilt and frustration build inside of her. She knew this was her fault. Had she not been so stubborn and adamant about getting into town and then getting to the house, none of this would have happened. He would still be alive.

She started down the slippery slope. She stopped when she saw the door open and the police officer tumble out carrying a flashlight and a large bag. He looked dazed and dizzy as he got to his feet and began climbing up.

"Oh my God, are you okay?" she yelled, seeing him struggling to get up the mucky embankment. His rain slicker was ripped and his clothes were muddy and saturated. "Hey, are you okay?" she repeated louder, reaching down to help him. "Grab my hand."

"Get back in your car," he ordered, motioning her away.

Ignoring his warnings, she started down the slope to help him. "I'm sorry. I just needed to get to my dad's house. I know this is my fault. Here, let me help you." She slipped as the mud beneath her feet gave way.

"No, go back," he warned, seeing her regain her balance. "This whole area could flood and wash away, go get back in your car."

"No, I can't just get back in the car and leave you here like this. Come on, take my hand."

"I'm fine," he insisted, just before slipping down the muddy slope. She reached down to him, but he motioned her away again. "Get back in your car now." He continued climbing until he neared the top of the slope. She grabbed his upper arm, but he winced and jerked away.

"At least give me the flashlight and bag. Come on, I'm only trying to help you up," she said. He looked up at her, nodded, and then tossed the flashlight and bag. She caught them easily, put them aside then reached for him again.

She grabbed his hand as he reached for a tangle of roots. She felt him pull away from her again. There was a loud crack behind them. They turned and saw another huge branch fall onto the jeep. Losing his footing, he slid back down into the muddied trench.

"Will you let me help you now?" she yelled. He hesitated. "Come on, your jeep is under a tree and halfway down a ditch. It's getting worse out here and we need to get inside now."

He grabbed her hand and she pulled, helping him to the edge of the slope. They collapsed back into each other's arms, him practically on top of her as they lay exhausted and breathless on the side of the road. They took faces full of lashing rain as gusting wind sheared through them, whipping her flimsy windbreaker and his uniform. "Come on." They staggered to their feet, picked up the supplies and hurried to her car still idling a few yards away. "We need to get to a shelter," he yelled above the high winds.

She turned, seeing there was no way they could get back the way they came. "The tree's blocking the road. We can't get through. We can go to my father's house." As soon as they got into her car, she sped away.

"What are you doing here?" he asked before thinking. "You're not supposed to be here, not now."

"Yeah, yeah, I know I'm stubborn. You told me to go back to the highway and I didn't. I needed to see for myself that the clerk's office was closed. But none of that matters now. We need to get out of this mess."

That wasn't what Stephen meant, but thankfully she understood him differently. He expected her to come down to the Keys and see about her father's house. He didn't expect her to risk life and limb to come in the middle of a hurricane. Leo was definitely right. His daughter was just as stubborn as he was.

"I hope we don't run into any more falling trees," Mia said, then glanced over to see his torn raincoat and uniform and the deep-red trail down his arm. "Oh my God, your arm. You're bleeding. I need to get you to a hospital." She slammed on the brakes and prepared to turn around.

"No, keep going. I'm fine," he muttered, still winded.

She continued driving. "But you're bleeding."

"I'm fine. I just need to call in." He pressed a knob on the walkie-talkie at his shoulder, but got only static.

"Is it broken?" Mia asked.

"No, it's the hurricane. The signals are out all over the Keys. The police band has been having problems all day. Do you have a cell phone?"

"There," she said, motioning to the cell phone attached to the car's cradle. "Use my phone."

He nodded, pressed the Call button then dialed. He pressed End, then dialed again. "There's no service."

The storm seemed to intensify a notch. The windshield wipers struggled against the wind and it was near impossible to see just a few yards ahead.

"It's getting worse out here," he said through clenched teeth.

"For once I'm in complete agreement with you," she said, driving as quickly and safely as possible.

"We need to get inside," he muttered, slowly closing his eyes and leaning his head back.

"We will," Mia said, sparing a quick glance at her passenger. His eyes were closed and he was breathing slow and deep. "Hey, don't fall asleep on me. You might have a concussion or something. We're almost there. My dad's friend is a doctor. He never leaves during a hurricane."

She managed to find the neighborhood with no problem, even though it was much different than she remembered.

Most of the homes in the area had been small tin-roofed bungalows, undersize eclectic-styled conch homes or simple colorful gingerbread cottages. They seemed to be all gone, replaced or rebuilt into elaborate mansion-styled tributes to wealth and privilege. She drove to her father's neighbor's house, passing beneath the row of bending palms swaying in the gusting winds.

She ran to the front door and knocked, then banged, but got no response. When she got back to the car, her passenger was unconscious.

She spared him a quick glance. He seemed very familiar for some reason. Did she know him?

She touched him gently. "Wake up. You have to stay awake."

"Mi fantasía, usted está aquí," he mumbled.

She translated easily. "My fantasy is here. What does that mean?" A loud crash of thunder sounded, and she jumped. Beside her, the officer woke up.

"Where are we?" he asked drowsily.

"I stopped at my dad's friend's house. He's a retired doctor, Dr. Russell, but he's not here."

"Jim Russell stays at the hospital during hurricanes. His medical expertise is needed there."

"Oh, okay, then we'll be at my dad's house in a minute." She shifted gears and continued driving. A few miles later she pulled into her father's modest driveway. Compared to the other homes she passed, his, now hers, was a pathetic reminder and relic from the past.

It was a small two-bedroom conch house built in the

late sixties. With a surrounding porch and yard out back, it sat high up on a ridge with wooden steps leading down toward the beach area. Nothing about the property had changed, except for the portion of the white picket fence that had been ripped down. The roof on the wrap-around porch had been badly damaged, and one hurricane shutter hung precariously.

Half windblown, half exhausted, they grabbed flashlights and a bag each, got out and then ran to the steps. She juggled her keys, and then finally opened the front door. A strong gust of wind took it, blowing it wide, slamming it against the inside wall. He grabbed it quickly as she hurried inside. "Come on in," she said. He followed, securing the door behind them.

"Man, it's crazy out there," she said breathlessly, walking into the living room and looking around in the darkness. She tried to turn on the table lamp she'd remembered by the sofa and realized it was no longer there. She moved to the light switch on the wall and toggled it a few times. Nothing happened. "There's no electricity," she said, checking a few more light switches.

"We're having rolling power outages to help conserve electricity. It'll probably continue for the next few days."

"It's sweltering in here. We need some air."

Closed up for months, the room was hot and stuffy. She moved to the separate air-ventilation system, hoping they still worked. They didn't. She turned back to him as thunder roared and the wind howled outside. He hadn't moved. He just stood there looking around as if waiting for something. "It's okay, it's my dad's house. He died a few months ago."

"Yes, I know. Leo James," he said softly, turning his flashlight on and upward to resemble a lantern.

"That's right." She looked at him surprised that he knew that. "You knew my father?"

He nodded and half smiled, showing a deep-set dimple in his right cheek. He sat the flashlight on the small table she didn't remember being there years ago. "Yeah, you could say something like that. We had history," he said, standing in the familiar house he knew all too well. He'd spent a lot of time here before Leo died.

Mia looked at him, puzzled by the cryptic remark. "Well, since it looks like we're going to be stuck here for a while, I guess we should introduce ourselves. I'm Mia," she said, moving toward him and extending her hand.

"I know," he said softly. "Stephen." He extended his hand. As soon as they shook she saw him wobble. She opened her mouth to say something, but he cut her off quickly. "There's a gas generator in the back. I'll check it." He took two steps then staggered and balanced himself against the wall.

"Whoa. No way. You need to sit down."

"No, I'm fine," he said, swaying again as he pushed away from the wall.

She grabbed him quickly, fearing he'd fall. Holding him tight, she moved him to the sofa. "You're not fine. Your arm is bleeding and so is your forehead. Sit down," she said firmly, helping him sit and lie back. She grabbed the flashlight and brought it closer. In the muted light she saw that the cut on his forehead didn't look as bad as she thought, but his arm, covered with mud and blood, was still bleeding badly. She sat on the edge of the coffee table in front of him. "I need to see how badly you're hurt. You need to take your clothes off," she said, but then realized how it sounded.

"You want me to take my clothes off?" he asked half smiling, and then he closed his eyes and lay back.

"No, that's not what I meant."

"Are you sure?" he asked.

"Positive. I meant that you need to take off your jacket and shirt. I need to see your arm. It's bleeding."

He nodded but didn't move. Realizing that he might be hurt worse than either of them realized, she leaned in and helped him remove his jacket. She struggled to get it over his arm, but finally got it off. Tossing it aside, she began unbuttoning his shirt. Her hands, usually steady and sure, trembled slightly. She slowly opened his shirt and began pulling it from his pants. She unbuckled his belt for easier access, but hesitated when her hand accidentally brushed against him. She instantly retreated and stood up.

"Um, you need to lean forward," she whispered. He did, resting his body against her. She inhaled deeply, reached down behind him and pulled his shirt from his pants. He raised his arm and she pulled his shirt off. She felt his hand hold on to her hips as she gently pulled it away from his other arm. There was something innately sensual about his head cradled against her that sent tingles through her body. This wasn't supposed to be seductive, but it sure felt that way.

"Okay," she began as she slowly sat down again. Face-to-face, she gazed down at his chest and unconsciously licked her lips. "Okay, um," she said again, forgetting what she was supposed to do. Stephen leaned in closer. Her focus shifted to his eyes. She knew what was coming. "Um," she said again, as their lips came closer. He leaned in and so did she, and in seconds their lips met tenderly. Then, with added pressure, the kiss deepened. It consumed her just long enough for her to realize that the attraction was very, very real.

She leaned back first. "Um, I gotta get you bandaged up." She saw that there was a blood-stained bandage already on his upper arm near his shoulder. "So you are hurt."

"It's an old wound," he said.

"It must not be that old because it's bleeding again. Do you still have stitches?" she asked. He shook his head. "I need to find the first aid kit and some more light. I'm sure my dad has something around here somewhere." She stood, looking around.

"There's a flashlight and a first aid kit in the kitchen cabinet under the sink. And the candles are on the top shelf on the left," Stephen said weakly, then closed his eyes and lay back.

She nodded, surprised that he knew that. What else did he know about the house and just how well had he known her father? she wondered. Were they close? And did he know about her, their strained relationship? Her father would guffaw at that word. He'd say, *strained* was a coward's way of saying she turned her back on him when he needed her most.

She rummaged through her purse, grabbed her cell phone then hurried into the kitchen. As soon as she walked in she looked around and smiled. It was like a time capsule. She dialed Janelle's phone number and prayed she'd get a signal as she began searching in the cabinets for supplies. Luckily, the call went through.

"You didn't call. What happened?" Janelle said, as soon as she picked up.

"Yeah, sorry, the phone keeps going in and out and then I kinda got distracted."

"Everything taken care of?" she asked.

"Not exactly," Mia said, glancing back at the unconscious cop on her father's sofa.

"What does that mean? Did you get the reprieve or not?"

"No, the office was closed because of the storm. I'm at my dad's house. We needed to get inside."

"Oh Lord, how is it down there?"

"It's about as you'd expect and worse. Torrential rain going sideways, blustering high winds and general craziness and insanity," she whispered.

"Mia, why are you whispering? And you said *we* needed to get inside—who's the we?" she asked.

"There's an unconscious deputy sheriff lying on the sofa in the living room."

"Why is there a cop lying on the sofa, Mia? What happened? Are you okay? Are you in trouble?"

"No, I'm fine, and it's a long story."

"Shorten it and tell me," Janelle insisted. Mia told Janelle about being stopped and the tree falling and the officer's injuries. "Tell me about the cuts and injuries," she asked. Mia did, so glad she had a doctor for a sister. "Okay, by your description the cuts and bruises don't sound life threatening, but it does sound like he might have a slight concussion. How long has he been unconscious?"

"Not long. He was talking earlier about being tired."

"I can't diagnose him over the phone, Mia, but I can walk you through some basic first aid until you can get him to medical attention." She told Mia what to do and what to look for.

"Okay, but I don't know about getting him to medical attention anytime soon. It's pretty bad out there."

"Fine, then you'll just have to do your best."

"I don't think he has a concussion. I think he's just sleepy and tired."

"What makes you say that?"

"He kissed me."

"He what?" Janelle asked.

"He kissed me. It was an accident I'm sure—I mean he was probably delirious or something—but still, he kissed me."

"Okay, we'll talk about that later. For right now see if you can keep him talking and focused. Ask him questions."

"What kind of questions?"

"Start general, day of the week, state, things like that. If he's answering correctly then just ask him about his family or his job. Most people will talk about that. It should keep him awake and alert. Check his eyes from time to time and also keep a close eye on that cut on his forehead. Make sure it doesn't start bleeding again."

"Anything else?" Mia asked.

"I'm on my way to Nya's house. Call us later."

"Electricity is out and I never connected the house phone. My cell needs charging and the signal is weak. I can barely hear you now."

"All right, try calling as soon as you can and we'll keep trying to call you, too. Be safe."

"I will and, Janelle, thanks for not saying I told you so."

"I learned a long time ago that you're just too stubborn to take anybody's word for anything. You had to see for yourself that the place was closed."

"Tell Nya I'm fine. I'll try to call you later."

Before Janelle replied, the signal was lost.

She began gathering the supplies she needed—
candles, two flashlights and the first aid kit. Thankfully there was running water, as per Janelle's
directions, she washed her hands thoroughly, poured
warm water into a large pot, grabbed clean towels
and took everything back to the sofa. She turned on
the two flashlights and lit several candles and placed
them around the room. By the time she sat down on
the coffee table across from him, she realized that he
was out cold.

"Officer, Stephen," she said, gently shaking his good
shoulder. He moaned, but only half woke up. "Hey,
remember me? Mia, the woman with the two fallen trees."

He smiled. "Mia, how could I forget you?" he asked
sincerely.

"Yeah, I'm sorry about all that. But I'm glad you
remember me. That's a good sign. I spoke to my sister.
She's a doctor and she said that I need to keep you
talking just in case you have a concussion."

"I don't have a concussion," Stephen said sleepily.
"I'm fine, just tired. I'm on light duty, but I pulled a
triple shift."

"Because of the storm?"

He nodded. "Hurricane evacuation."

"Oh, okay, but why are you on light duty before?"

"There was an accident. I helped some people and
then I got hurt myself."

"So you're a superhero, huh?"

"No, just doing my job," he muttered slowly,
closing his eyes.

"Hey, wake up," she said, gently stroking his face.
The slight stubble felt soft to the touch. "You need to
stay with me awhile longer."

"I'll stay with you forever," he whispered.

She smiled remembering his kiss. "Careful, Officer, I might just hold you to that."

"Promise," he said, opening his eyes and watching her as she began taking items out of the first aid kit beside her. Then she carefully removed the old bandage on his arm, wet a towel and began gently cleaning the wound, removing dried mud and blood.

"So, Stephen, do you always flirt with women you meet in hurricanes?"

"No, just you, Mia, only you."

"And why is that, Officer?"

"Because you're the woman I want."

"But you don't even know me."

"I know you," he said simply.

Mia looked into his eyes. The stark seriousness in his expression quietly stunned her. She was sure he was joking, but his eyes were so genuine. "Um, so, do you know what a concussion feels like?" she asked, hoping to end the uneasy feeling of attraction snaking through her stomach.

"Yes," he said, smiling.

"Oh really, is that right?" she asked skeptically. He nodded. She looked into his dark eyes. They were glassy, but as he said, he looked more tired than confused. "Why are you smiling?" she asked him.

"Because you're finally here," he said as he reached up and touched her face. "You're not a dream."

"So me being here with you makes you happy. I think maybe you do have a concussion after all." He closed his eyes and fell asleep, and she smiled, thinking how wonderful it would be to really have a man feel that way about her. She continued to clean his arm, relieved that the opened cut wasn't worse. She applied the anti-septic gel then several Band-Aid bandages.

Next, she checked the small cut on his forehead. It proved slightly more challenging than she expected. The cut wasn't too bad, but he'd rolled his head to the side and the awkward way he was lying made tending to the cut difficult. She had to nearly straddle his lap to clean it and apply the bandage. She gently, slowly turned his head to face her. Thunder rolled and he winced and moaned in his sleep.

She froze, expecting him to awaken and see her strad-dling him. But he didn't. He just moaned again and eased back further. She leaned in again, placing her knees astride his thighs. The physical proximity and sugges-tiveness of her position was obvious. Had he awoken at that moment she wasn't sure how she'd have explained.

She cleaned his cut and finished her task quickly. Standing, she looked down at her patient. He slept peacefully, so she decided to get some rest, too. Across the room she sat down in the large comfortable chair her father loved. She picked up his pipe in the ashtray on the side table. It still smelled of cherry tobacco, as did the flawed afghan she knitted one summer. She held the pipe to her nose and inhaled. It was her father. She looked up at the portrait of her and her father on the mantel. She'd been about thirteen at the time it had been taken. She smiled, then looked over to Stephen. It was obvious he knew her father well. She wondered just how well. Her father never mentioned Stephen to her, but of course, she hadn't exactly been around much the last few years.

Leonard James, her father, died nine months ago. He was a brilliant writer and a self-professed journalistic rebel. When it came to seeking the truth and reporting, he was unequalled. A Pulitzer Prize winner, he was cutting, candid and brutal with a satirical edge that angered a lot of people. But he didn't care. He wrote the truth as he saw it and never took his words back. He often said the truth hurt, and exposing corruption was supposed to hurt a lot. His motto was "no excuses, no retractions."

As a result he made enemies, a lot of enemies. Most he insisted on calling sore losers; others he called currently uncommitted felons. Investigative reporting was his life. He loved what he did and he was good at it. When he stopped writing years ago he became a different man.

The change in him was even more so evident when she brought Neal down to meet him. The two men got along like fire and water. Her father despised Neal instantly, which broke her heart. And when she told him that they were engaged, he was furious and threatened to boycott the wedding and disown her if she went through with it. In the end he was right about Neal. He turned out to be exactly what her father said he was.

She curled up, laid her head back and closed her eyes. Outside, the storm surged and the winds blew steadily as the rumble of thunder began to lull her. Inside, memories, both good and bad, flooded her consciousness. She was hard-pressed to determine which storm was more threatening.

Chapter 5

The blast of howling wind woke Mia up. She looked around, then peered at her watch. It was after midnight. The room had darkened as a few of the candles had melted down. She heard Stephen moan and went over to him. The bandage on his forehead had come loose. She leaned over to secure it. He moaned again. "Shh, it's okay, I just need to check your forehead again," she said gently. Without thinking, she straddled him as before and adjusted the bandage.

She began to notice his features more closely. She was right before, he did look familiar. His face was angular and chiseled and definitely model-perfect. His skin was sun-kissed with deep rich mocha and a mixture of racial backgrounds showed in his features. His eyes were closed now, but she remembered they were dark, almost black, now rimmed with long curly lashes. His mouth was sexy and sensuously full, the lips temptingly shaped, seemingly perfect for long, leisurely kisses and sweet, tender nibbles.

Unable to resist, she touched his lips then hesitated. What was she doing? Her grandmother would be aghast. Good girls didn't do this. Good girls didn't touch. Her libido must be in serious overdrive. The man was unconscious and she was fondling his body. Besides that, the man was a cop.

She checked the bandage one last time, then paused and just stared at him. Her searching eyes greedily devoured every inch of his face. Manly and strong, he was very attractive, more so than she originally considered. His mocha skin shimmered in the flickering candlelight. She placed her hands on his broad shoulders, feeling the magnificent iron muscles beneath.

He was solid, strong and powerful and she liked the feel of him. She began touching him, running her hands over his shoulders, to his arms, over his chest then downward. His muscles rippled tight from his chest to his open belt. She stroked the washboard stillness of his stomach. It was chiseled stone. She smiled at her guilty pleasure. She knew she shouldn't be doing this, but the temptation was just too strong. Besides, who would know? Her stomach trembled as she leaned in and touched her lips to his just once.

Leaning back, her skin goose-pimpled. She knew it was wrong but for some reason, it felt so right. She leaned in again. This time her kiss was longer. This time it was also different. This time he kissed back.

Surprised, she jumped back. The penetrating intensity of his dark sexy eyes sent instant shivers through her body. "Oh my God, I'm sorry, that was so wrong," she said, moving farther away. He held her in place. "I don't know what came over me, I just—I've never done anything like that before. I don't know what I was thinking. I was— I never lose control like that."

His hand reached out to her in almost slow motion. His body tensed as his jaw and stomach muscles tightened. He touched her face tenderly and smiled. "Mia, *mi fantasía,* maybe you should lose control more often." His hand gently cradled then cupped her neck, drawing her close. Her lips were still parted in awe when he captured her mouth. Kissing her full, deep and with promise, he literally took her breath away. He delved deep into her mouth, his tongue circling playfully, tasting her sweetness. Seconds later, his arms wrapped around her, holding her close as she collapsed against him.

She moaned, melting against his body, feeling the rhythm of her heartbeat accelerate. He held her close, guiding her across his lap. She felt her body moisten and it had nothing to do with the room's stagnant heat. *My God, what is this man doing to me?* The sweet kiss turned quickly into a heart-pounding, nerve-numbing, toe-curling, erotic experience. Her thoughts swam dizzily as she wrapped her arms around his neck and positioned herself to take him in fully.

She leaned forward, pressing her breasts against him, pinning his back against the pillows. Her nipples hardened as they crushed into him. His hands encircled her tighter, pulling her buttocks closer against his unmistakable desire. She felt him, hard and ready, pressing between her legs. He wanted her and she wanted him. The sensation of feeling him hard for her was too arousing to deny and she ground her hips into him. Her thoughts spun wildly. She was floating, losing balance, swept up in the blissful passion of the moment.

His tongue penetrated deep into her mouth, rubbing and tickling the roof of her mouth. She shivered. This was different; he was different. She'd never felt the pull of passion and desire so intensely. The sensation was beyond imaginable. She was losing control.

She closed her eyes, savoring his mouth on her body. He kissed her hard and long, then trailed his lips to her neck, her shoulder and chest, nibbling, licking, sucking, sending tremors through every nerve ending. She moaned and arched back, giving him full access to her body. Desire welled in her stomach and heated her blood.

Suddenly an unexpected chill enveloped as a memory assailed her. *"Sexually repressed."* Neal's comment echoed in her mind. What if she disappointed Stephen, too? She couldn't take another embarrassment. She knew she had to stop or be humiliated. She needed to regain control. "Wait, wait," she rasped, pushing back from him, surprised to see her shirt was open and she was literally on top of him, straddling him. He nodded and released her instantly.

"Maybe we should slow down," she muttered, breathlessly. "I know this seems like I'm teasing, but believe me, I'm not. It's just that— I mean, I don't know anything about you. You could be married or engaged, or—"

He interrupted. "Mia, I'm not married, I'm not engaged or anything else."

"Still, you're a cop and I just about molested you, when you were unconscious no less. Talk about coming on strong. I can't believe I did that," she said.

He held her secure for one last moment. "In case you

hadn't noticed, I'm not complaining," he assured her tenderly. He released her and she quickly began buttoning her shirt, then gathering the discarded bandages and other trash from the table.

"The thing is," she began, and then a loud crash got their attention. The boom was followed by a tremor as the small house shook.

Chapter 6

"I think it came from out back," Mia exclaimed.

Stephen stood and grabbed his shirt and flashlight, then headed straight to the sound, through the kitchen to the back door. Grabbing another flashlight, Mia followed close behind him. He opened the back door to find that a sizable tree branch had split and fallen into the house, nearly breaking off one of the hurricane shutters which now hung loose. He stepped out farther. The wind whipped furiously around him as he tried to move the branch away from the house and secure the shutter. "Take this," he bellowed, handing her the shirt and flashlight. "Go back inside."

"No, don't," Mia yelled over the loud winds. "We can't do anything about it now. I'll take care of it later."

"No, I need to secure the shutter now or flying debris might hit and break the window."

She nodded and then stepped outside and watched as he began to move the large branch. His strong arms were thick bands of muscle glistening in the rain. He grabbed the branch, held firm, and then heaved it back. His biceps clinched and his stomach tightened. Even though the rain had eased a bit, he was still getting soaked and all she could think about was how good it would feel to continue what they started a few minutes ago. "Um, I'll help," she called out, hoping to distract the lustful hunger she was feeling.

"No, go back inside," he instructed, "I got this." Ignoring him, she rushed to his side and began tugging at the branch. Together they moved it away from the house and he turned his attention to securing the shutter. "Hold this," he told Mia as he indicated the dangling shutter. "I need to get a hammer and some nails." He ran back into the house.

Mia held the corner of the shutter, looking at her shaking hands. She wasn't sure if it was the storm or the thought of him causing them to shake. The winds beat at her back and a deluge of rain from the roof poured down near her. For the first time in her life she was losing control. Everything she thought was tangled up in wayward emotions. Her grandmother always told her to never lose herself. She never had, not until lately. She was in a hurricane, losing her father's house and all she could think about was making love to a man she just met. She didn't even know his last name.

A loud crash startled her and she looked behind her. The wooden picnic table had overturned and slammed against the back fence. But beyond that the sight was horrendous. The yard was a disaster. High winds had uprooted several bushes and ripped shingles from the shed's roof. There were deck chairs tossed against the fence and debris was scattered everywhere. The first thing she thought was that her father would be devastated. The yard was his joy.

Stephen came back with a hammer and nails and secured the loose shutter. The fix was temporary, but it seemed good enough for the time being. She gave him his shirt and then watched as he put it on, leaving it unbuttoned. It blew chaotically with the blustering wind. "Why don't you go back in the house?" he said as the rain sprayed his face. "I'm gonna check the rest of the shutters and windows."

She shook her head. "I need to get my bags from the car," she said. He nodded. She followed him as he hurried around to each side of the house looking up at the windows. They were covered by shutters and seemed secure. When they got to the front of the house, she hurried to the car and grabbed her two suitcases. He rushed over and took them from her and then grabbed his duffel bag. They ran back into the kitchen, winded and wet.

"It sounds like the hurricane's getting closer. Are you okay?" he asked.

Breathing heavily, she half smiled and nodded. "I'm hot and I'm wet." The tremble of her voice was low and sexy and that was all he needed for his body to want her all over again. "I think it's going to be a long night," she added.

"I think you're right."

Then suddenly the living room lights came on.

"Hey, the electricity is back on," she said. "Maybe the worst will be over soon."

Stephen looked at her and his breath caught in his throat. Instinctively his body reacted as his eyes burned a trail down her body. He didn't respond right away. He didn't expect the sight of her to arouse him so completely. Her shirt was half-open and the damp swell of her breasts caught his eye. His mouth went dry as he tried to lick his lips. The cotton shirt was soaked and sticking to her easily visible lace bra. The top few buttons were still undone from earlier and the thought of licking the moisture from her chest was too tempting. Whether unintentionally or not, she was pure seduction.

He looked away. "I don't think so," he muttered in response to her remark. He needed a distraction. "Uh, the shutters down here look fine, but I need to double check the windows upstairs and in the attic."

She nodded. "Okay, I'll go with you," she said.

"No, stay here," he said abruptly, and then turned.

"But—" she began, he was already walking away. She followed him into the living room, then stopped and watched him go upstairs. She couldn't help but admire the view from behind. Broad shoulders, narrow waist and legs just bowed enough to be sexy as he walked. Dragging herself away, she began extinguishing the candles and then turned off the flashlights.

As she did, she looked around, reminiscing. The house, with its distinct characteristics, was painted a musty tan with traces of the festive lavender she'd loved so much when she was a child. She remembered the summer they'd painted it together. She'd been thirteen and it had taken them most of their time together to do it, but by the time it was done she was over the moon thrilled. It had been pink and lavender, just like the dollhouse he'd sent her the Christmas before.

She smiled, remembering the following summer she came to visit. She'd expected the house to be exactly as she'd painted it, but it wasn't. He'd changed the pink to tan. He apologized, telling her that he just couldn't live in a pink house any longer. But he kept the purple and that was all that mattered.

Suddenly she realized just how much she loved this house. It was cluttered and junky but it had character that stemmed from classic Victorian mixed insanely with Caribbean Island influences. Of course the dream of the house was much different than the reality. In reality the possibility of collapse due to neglect seemed plausible. Now frayed and tattered, it was no longer an ode to her father, but instead to their time together. She supposed that was what she wanted to save more than anything else. Holding on to this house meant holding on to him.

More resolved than ever, she decided not to give up. She knew she needed to do this. After everything that had passed between her and her father, and especially the last few years, she needed to do this for him.

She sat down in the large chair, looking at the sofa across from her. The memory of lying there with Stephen, running her hands down his chest, and kissing started to heat her skin. Her stomach quivered then did a somersault. She took a deep breath and released it slowly. Maybe it was a bad idea for her to stay down here.

Stephen had hurried upstairs, doubling the last four steps to expedite his ascent. He needed to put as much distance between the two of them as soon as possible. The earlier taste and feel of her had started a chain reaction that had put his body in permanent standby. Seeing her standing there earlier in the kitchen soaking wet nearly sent him over the top. He wanted her, but that wasn't what he was supposed to do.

Needing a momentary distraction, he busied himself by checking the windows in the bedrooms. They were all secure. Afterward he headed to the attic. As soon as he got to the doorway he saw Mia standing at an open window. He entered softly. Rain and wind blustered in, blowing dust and loose papers around the attic. "You need to get away from the window," he told her. She didn't answer, "Mia," he called softly. She turned as he approached. He took her hand and gently pulled her away, then closed and secured the window and hurricane shutters.

"It's hot. It feels like a sauna in here," she said warily.

"Yeah, hot. You have no idea," he muttered absently, busing himself with a stubborn shutter latch. "I thought you were going to wait downstairs."

She smiled and shrugged. "I guess I didn't want to be alone," she said quietly.

Stephen nodded. Still feeling the need for distance, he checked the other windows and shutters while keeping an eye on Mia as she walked and looked around.

"It's funny, I haven't been up here in years and now all I can think about is how much my dad loved working up here." She ran her finger along the edge of his big desk, making a trail in the dust. She smiled thoughtfully. "I'd play up here for hours while he typed." She looked around seeing all the storage boxes against the back wall. "Man, look at all this stuff." She walked over and opened the closest box and peeked inside. She took out an oddly shaped ashtray. "Oh, my gosh, I can't believe he actually kept this. I made this for Father's Day when I was nine years old."

Stephen leaned back against the desk and watched

her. The sparkling glint in her eyes was unmistakable. She ran her fingers over every dent and crack, then turned it upside down and read the inscription. She smiled, looking more sexy and desirable than ever. "I think Leo liked to keep things," he said.

She looked up. Their eyes connected as they stood in the muted darkness under the one overhead light. At that moment the familiarity of his face seemed more apparent. "You know, I think I remember you—from the memorial service. You were the cop who was with him when he died, aren't you?" Stephen nodded. "I looked for you after the service, but you were gone."

"I had to leave."

"Thank you," she said softly, "for what you did for him."

"It was my pleasure."

"And about what happened downstairs, or rather what almost happened...I don't know what I was thinking."

"Again, my pleasure," he joked.

They smiled. The suggestive remark seemed to add to the already sexually charged air around them. She looked into his piercing dark eyes and the room got even hotter. She turned away, distracting herself. "So, I wonder what's in all these boxes."

Stephen walked over and stood beside her. "Leo told me that he kept everything he ever wrote, his journals, letters, memos, drafts, even a few bad detective novels and of course his acceptance speech for Stockholm, Sweden."

"Stockholm?" she asked.

"He told me once that he expected to win a Nobel Prize for Literature and didn't want to leave the acceptance speech until the last minute."

"He told you that?" She smiled. "It sounds just like him. He was always so sure of himself."

"Yeah, his confidence was unrivaled."

Mia laughed. "If you mean he was cocky and stubborn, you're right. Most people he wrote about called his confidence pigheaded arrogance. I heard that there was this one man who even threatened to make him disappear after a particularly scathing investigative article. I think it had something to do with faulty construction material. But my dad refused to retract a single word. I think he just loved a good fight." Stephen didn't reply so she continued. "So you knew him pretty well, I guess. Were you one of his informants or something like that?"

"No, nothing that dramatic."

"How did you meet him?"

"Most recently, I arrested him."

"You arrested my father?" she said, surprised. "When? Why?"

"The when was about a year and a half ago. The why was for disorderly conduct and public drunkenness."

"Figures," she said bitterly.

"Why would you say that?"

"I don't know if you knew him before, but my dad changed a few years ago. He quit his job and refused to write another word for publication."

"Do you know why?" he asked.

"No, but I have my suspicions. Something major happened to make him stop. He never told me what it was. He gave me the standard excuse—he'd had enough—but I didn't buy it. He loved investigative journalism too much. He always told me to never give up, never surrender to pressure. And the thing is he gave up on himself and started drinking." She looked away sadly.

Stephen saw her pained expression but didn't respond. Apparently she didn't know the whole truth about her father and he knew this wasn't the time or place to reveal it to her. Instead he told her about the night they'd met.

"He didn't usually drink. I think he was hurting that night and decided to throw a party for himself in the middle of Main Street. Actually, I didn't technically arrest him that time. It was more like taking him someplace to sleep it off. I think he'd had a particularly bad day."

She smiled. "My mom always said that my dad used to have a lot of bad days when they were married. Then he went on the wagon. I guess he fell off."

"Leo was a good man. He just had a few limitations."

She chuckled. "Limitations—that's putting it nicely. Most people thought he was an egotistical, big-headed bastard. My mom was one of them. He drove people crazy, and then he drove them away."

"Did he drive you away?"

"He wanted me to dump my ex-fiancé, but I wouldn't. I should have, because he was right about him. But that's a different story. I just wish we…" She didn't finish. Instead, she looked away quickly. It wasn't her father that drove her away. It was her stubbornness to be right that ended their closeness. Maybe Neal was right. Maybe she was cold and controlling. "My dad and I weren't close when he died. I guess you knew that, though. Circumstance separated—" she began then halted, swallowing hard and feeling her pain choke her.

"He adored you," he said gently.

"And you know that how?" she asked.

"The way he talked about you."

"He talked about me?" she asked.

"Nonstop," he said, standing in front of her.

"Why didn't he tell me how sick he was?"

"He loved you too much."

Tears hidden for so long pushed forward, but Mia refused to release them. She didn't cry before and she wasn't going to cry now. Crying was for the weak. She had to be strong and stay in control. But it was getting harder and harder to do when every part of her wanted to just let go and give in.

"Mia," Stephen said softly, taking her hand. "Hey, are you okay?" She nodded, but it was obvious that she wasn't. "It's okay to let go."

"No, it's not."

He pulled her close, but she resisted. "Yes, it is. Believe me, you need this." Seconds later, she went willingly and for just a moment she let go and melted into his arms. He blanketed her with his strength. Her body shuddered as she closed her eyes, feeling safe and protected by a man she barely knew. They stood there a moment, feeling the closeness grow between them.

"Are you okay?" he asked again as he began stroking her back.

"Not even close," she said, nestling closer into his embrace. He held her loosely then kissed her forehead with a sweet promise. She closed her eyes, savoring his touch. He felt good, he smelled good and heaven help her, all she could think about was a half hour earlier when he'd tasted so very good.

The fortress she had so carefully erected around her heart began to show signs of weakness. She pressed her body closer and felt him react to her pressure. She nuzzled, sensing the readiness in both of them to take it one step further.

She leaned back and looked up at him. Their eyes connected. It was there, everything she ever wanted, right there in his eyes. The surging inferno reignited the smoldering burn inside her. Stephen must have felt it, too, because his hands traveled up her arms, to her shoulders then along the curve of her neck and jaw where they tipped up her chin slightly. Mia held her breath, expecting and wanting whatever came next. He leaned in closer, just inches from her mouth. The musky scent of his body enveloped her, and she wallowed in its richness. His heated breath mingled with her own, making her stomach spin in circles. *Kiss me,* she wanted to scream. *Touch me, take me.*

"You're closer than you think," he whispered ominously, as if it were a promise of things to come and not just a hopeful suggestion.

The essence of his breath was so close she could almost taste it. Her heart pounded and every nerve ending tingled. No one, especially Neal, had ever made her feel this level of intensity of excitement and desire. Everything about this moment felt so right. She couldn't believe she was doing this, but desire pulled too strong to resist.

Finally his mouth descended on hers, lightly, barely covering hers, giving her latitude to step back. She didn't. She couldn't. Her arousal soared too high. She wanted this. She wanted him.

Her lips parted and his tongue playfully entered her mouth. The burn was there, icy and hot, lightning quick and torturously slow. He moved inside of her and all she could think was, more. She wrapped her arms around him, sealing her hungry kiss to his lips. There was no time, no place, no hurricane pounding to enter their cocoon of ecstasy. There was only the two of them in a dusty attic joined for as long as the kiss lasted.

Somewhere in the back of her mind she started to think again. The icy fog of panic thickened, slicing through the warmth. Good Lord, what was wrong with her? He was being caring and compassionate and all she could think was how good it felt to be in his arms. Apparently reading all those books had finally driven her sex crazy, or at the very least horny as all get-out. After a deep breath she took control then leaned back, putting much needed distance between them. "Um, I'm better," she said, lacking genuine assurance.

"Maybe not yet, but you will be."

She stepped back further and looked at him. His dark sexy eyes were glassy and his face was tense and stressed. "You don't look so good. Maybe you'd better go back downstairs and rest."

"I'm fine. I just need to wash up," he said.

"Oh, sure, there's a bathroom downstairs, second door—"

"—On the left. Yes, I know. But I think I'll just go down and wash up in the mudroom. I'll check on the generator while I'm there." He walked past her toward the stairs.

"Sure," Mia said, pivoting slightly, just enough to watch him walk away and climb down the steps. She bit her lip in ardent admiration of his tall, broad shoulders, tight rear and narrow waist. The man had a hell of a sexy walk. Immediately, the image of him shirtless came to mind, followed closely by the feel of his hardness pressed assuredly against her stomach. The attic, already sweltering, got even hotter.

Mia grabbed a folder from on top of one of the boxes and fanned herself. She leaned back, half sitting against the edge of the desk while looking back down the empty hall. Stephen was long gone, but the mere thought of him made her stomach quiver. She wondered what might have happened had she not stopped herself earlier.

"Hot, butt-naked sex would have happened," she whispered.

The off-the-wall, out-of-character, Nya-like comment made her smile. There was no way her stepsister would have backed off. She'd have enjoyed every minute of him, using every one of her books to illustrate exactly what she wanted him to do to her. Mia blushed. Bold wasn't her. She'd read the books Nya had sent her, but there was no way she could do half the things it listed. Could she?

Suddenly the idea of practicing what she'd read the last few months made her curious. Having meaningless sex with a willing partner was probably exactly what she should do. Neal called her cold, frigid and sexually repressed, but she knew she wasn't. Being with Stephen was proving it. Maybe now was the time to put all her newly acquired knowledge into practice. Stephen just might be the perfect practice subject.

Once again a quick retreat was the only thing Stephen could think to do. Seeing Mia standing there wet and tempting was killing him. Touching her, holding her, kissing her, feeling their bodies pressed too close wasn't going to work. He wanted her too much. It was the second time that evening they'd come close. He didn't realize how difficult this would be. But he gave his word and he intended to keep his promise.

He stood in the center of the mudroom. His body was still tense, his heart still pounded and it had nothing to do with the storm outside. It was Mia, his Mia, the woman he'd been dreaming about for months. The woman Leo talked about for a year, the woman who had no idea who he really was and what he really wanted. This had gone beyond turning into a simple attraction; it was a near obsession.

Women had never been a problem for him. He loved them and they loved him. Although he'd never been particularly serious with any one woman, he'd had more than a few romances in his time. Yet none of them was serious enough to even consider that long walk down the aisle.

His last date was with an attractive woman. She was smart, funny and sexy. They had dinner, hung out and then she suggested they return to his place. For the first time in his life he turned a woman down. All he kept thinking about the entire evening was Mia. He wrongly compared her to Mia, or better yet his idea of Mia.

He clenched his fists and slowly licked his lips, hoping to taste the last remnants of her kiss. She was sweet and luscious and everything he'd imagined she'd be. He could only imagine tasting the rest of her body. Every fantasy he'd had in the past few months had come back to taunt him. She came, just as he knew she would and she was just as intoxicating as he imagined.

Even now, moments later, he was swept up in his passion of wanting her. He turned to the large mirror over the sink. His weathered face looked back at him. Fighting for control over his passion, he turned on the faucet and splashed cold water on his face. It helped, but he needed more than this. He removed his shirt, grabbed a towel and washed up in ice-cold water.

In a few minutes he would walk back out there and his fantasy would be waiting for him. He was getting aroused again just thinking about her. He splashed more cold water on his face. The icy splash made him shudder as it ran down his neck to his chest.

He blamed Leo for this. For months as he recuperated, he talked about nothing else. Mia was his heart and the one thing that he said he'd done right in his life. At first Stephen just listened to an old man's ramblings, and then he slowly began to take a greater interest. He asked questions about Mia, and Leo was more than willing to answer. Slowly she'd become a dream, then a fantasy, then the unattainable woman of his desires. And now she was here.

But none of this was supposed to happen. He'd promised Leo that he'd watch the house until Mia arrived, then he'd watch out for her when she came. He never expected that she'd stay on his mind for the last nine months. The result was that he'd fallen for her and meeting her only added to his deepening feelings. He cupped and splashed more cold water, dried off and grabbed clean clothes from his bag.

He dressed in a T-shirt and sweats, but lingered in the mudroom longer than necessary. He needed time to think. Never in his fantasies had he imagined being with Mia in the middle of a hurricane. He saw Leo's old generator boxed against the far wall. He went over, pulled it out and busied himself with a distraction. Unfortunately, Mia still stayed on his mind.

Chapter 7

She tried her cell, and surprisingly, the call went through. "Well, it's about time you called," Nya said. "What happened? We expected to hear from you hours ago. We even tried to call you, but the call didn't go through."

"I'm here, too," Janelle said, picking up the extension at Nya's house. "What's going on?"

"I'm fine. I'm here at the house. The phones are having problems because of the storm. You're fading in and out. I can barely hear you," Mia answered.

"What happened with the cop? Did you get him medical attention?" Janelle asked.

"No, actually, he's still here. He's better."

"Janelle told me about your new hurricane friend. Is he cute?" Nya asked.

"Nya," both Janelle and Mia said.

"I'm just saying. Look, Mia's been on and on about

wanting to change her life and shake it up. She's been reading all those books so maybe it's time to do a road test."

"Nya," they repeated.

"Well, this might be a possible start. That's if he's at least physically attractive."

"Oh, he is attractive, very attractive."

"In that case, you can get started tonight. Find a chapter in the book and then just do it."

"It's not that easy, Nya, at least not for me. I can't just walk up to a man, rip his clothes off and jump him."

"It's easier than you think, believe me. Did you pack the goodie bag I sent you?" Nya asked.

"Oh Lord, not the goodie bag," Janelle said, "What did you put in it?"

"Don't ask," Mia said, "and yes, I packed it, but I don't know what half the things are."

"Don't worry about that. You'll figure it out when the time comes," Nya said, chuckling.

"*If* the time comes," Mia stated firmly.

"Whoa, what about your master plan? In case you forgot, Ms. I'm-Tired-of-Being-Called-Frigid-and-I'm-Ready-to-Do-Something-About-It, you have a month-long bungalow on Paradise Island waiting for you. Not to mention a few dozen men to sex up."

Mia chuckled. Of her two stepsisters, Nya was by far the most outrageous.

"Nya," Mia chastised, "woman, you are too shameless."

Nya ignored her and continued. "No, I'm honest. White sand beaches, breathtaking sunsets, duty-free shopping and if that weren't enough, the place is brimming with drop-dead gorgeous island men every three feet."

"Well, she does have a point there," Janelle added. "I wish I could get away from the clinic and go with you. I could use a few weeks off."

"Ditto," Nya added wishfully. "Hmm, weeks with nothing to do but sample the island's pleasures, shopping, men, food, men, shopping and more men." The three laughed at Nya's usual singled-minded focus. "I still can't believe what that jerk said to you," Nya added. "I get mad just thinking about it."

"Let's not even get into that again," Janelle said. "Mia, just remember to drink plenty of fluids and don't overdo it."

"What kind of advice is that?" Nya asked her sister. "Of course she should overdo it. She needs to overdo it, let loose, have fun and get that idiot man's stupid remarks out of her head. And Paradise Island is exactly the place to overdo it."

"I still can't believe you guys talked me into going."

"You need it, so just let go and enjoy," Nya advised.

"I hope you didn't send her anything too outrageous," Janelle said calmly. "Remember, Mia's not like you, Nya."

"Honey child, nobody's like me," Nya quipped provocatively.

"She's got a point there," Janelle added, chuckling.

"But there's nothing wrong with Mia picking up a few of my more interesting idiosyncrasies."

"What idiosyncrasies?" Mia asked knowingly.

Nya elaborated in full detail as Mia chuckled and listened to them continue discussing Nya's varying appetites. Her free-spirited personality was the exact opposite of Janelle's crusader personality, putting Mia right in the middle.

All said and done, Nya was right. There was nobody

like her. She was bold and brash, outspoken and opinionated. At twenty-eight, she was the managing editor of a national women's magazine and a celebrated publishing dynamo with enough clout to start her own successful publishing enterprise. Janelle, on the other hand, was more into service. At twenty-nine, she'd worked for the Peace Corps and Doctors Without Borders, garnered major awards and had just recently returned to open her own partnership practice.

Mia, at twenty-eight, was the exact opposite of both her stepsisters. As an English literature professor, she was far more introverted and reserved. Having grown up in Atlanta with her social maven grandmother, Mia was used to polite conversation and distant emotions. She kept everything bottled up inside, including her feelings. No wonder her ex-fiancé told her she had as much feeling as an iceberg.

The conversation eventually turned to more detailed Paradise Island adventures. Her sisters had visited the island the year before and stayed at Nya's bungalow. The stories they told when they returned were outrageous. There was no way Mia would ever do anything they suggested, yet the idea of testing her boundaries did intrigue her. But Mia only half listened. She was thinking about Stephen.

"Mia, I hope you're not using this as a way of backing out of this vacation like you did last year. You're not with Neal anymore, so there's no reason to back out."

"Not going last year had nothing to do with Neal. Well, mostly nothing. Anyway, I'm not backing out. I'm just postponing it a few days. I have every intention of leaving for Paradise Island as soon as this is over."

"Good," both Nya and Janelle said.

"So where are you now?" Janelle asked.

"In my old bedroom with a deputy sheriff downstairs changing his clothes," she said, knowing it would start a myriad of questions. It did. When she'd told them what had happened, their advice was simple: start her vacation early.

Chapter 8

By the time Mia came downstairs, Stephen had cleaned up and changed into a police T-shirt and sweats. He looked even more tempting than before. Maybe she was tired, maybe she was distracted, or maybe it was just exactly what she needed, but whatever it was, she was definitely feeling him. Actually, she was more than feeling him. She was hot for him. Everything he did, everything he said pushed her closer to wanting him more.

She stood a moment at the open mudroom doorway and just watched him as he worked. How many fantasies come to life like this? Mia wondered. This vacation was supposed to be about letting go and enjoying life and everything that came with it. She looked down at the man working diligently. Being timid had gotten her nowhere in the past. She needed to be bold, take what she wanted, and right now she wanted him. Even now, seeing him bent over trying to fix the generator had her nearly salivating.

"Hey," she said, interrupting his tinkering, "need a hand?"

He turned around and she smiled. According to the expression on his face she'd apparently chosen the perfect outfit. He looked her up and down, licked his lips then quickly looked away speechless. He obviously approved.

"Need a hand?" she repeated. He still didn't respond. She tilted her head questioningly as she moved closer. Maybe he didn't approve.

A halter top sundress got the deciding vote. It was the dress her stepsister Janelle had given her for her birthday, early bohemian with a generous sprinkling of erotic sex appeal. After a quick cool shower, she rifled through her bags and pulled it out. It was sexy without being too obvious, and the gossamer material was perfect for an island rendezvous. It was also just as perfect for a relaxed and comfortable evening at home. The idea of going barefoot with just her anklet and toe ring came from a chapter in her book. "Stephen?"

"Ah, no, no, I'm good," he finally said, turning around again. His expression was perfect. "You look nice," he said, then turned away.

She smiled. "Thanks, so do you. How's your arm and forehead? Need me to put on another bandage?"

"No, I took care of it," he tossed over his shoulder.

She moved closer, bending down beside him to get a better look at what he was doing. The fresh clean scent of his body was very enticing. She wholeheartedly approved. "So what exactly is wrong with it?" she asked.

"Besides needing gas, I don't have a clue. Mechanics isn't my forte."

She chuckled. "Obviously, any man comfortable enough to use the word *forte* isn't what I'd call a grease and oil kind of guy. But if it's any consolation, you look like you know what you're doing."

"Thanks."

She leaned in even closer. He obviously knew something about machinery because he had a few pieces disassembled and laid out on an old towel. "Doesn't that long screw fit inside that hole?"

"Yes."

"So why don't you screw it in?"

"I will, later."

"What's that part for?"

"Pumping action," he said.

Mia smiled and wondered if he noticed that the conversation had all the earmarks of a seduction scene. "Do you need a lubricant?" she added with a mischievous smile.

"No, I don't think so," he said, picking up a small mechanical part and attaching it to the unit.

"That's the engine, right? How powerful is it?"

"It's pretty powerful," he said.

"So why don't you just switch it on?"

"Some things need to be handled carefully."

"And some things need to just be turned on."

"It'll be worth the wait, trust me."

"Good, 'cause I'm looking forward to it."

He stopped working and smiled at her. Then they both laughed out loud. "Are we still talking about the generator?" he asked.

"I wondered if you noticed."

"Yeah, kind of hard not to," he said.

"Maybe I should go look for the manual."

"Better yet, it's late, so why don't you check the kitchen for something to eat? We might be here awhile."

She stood and took a few steps back. "Good idea." His back was to her, but she saw him shake his head. She went back into the kitchen and began opening cabinets. She found two cans of peaches, tuna fish, a half dozen bottles of water, a jar of marinated artichoke hearts and green olives. She pulled everything out and set it on the counter. It was a motley mixed dinner, but at this point making reservations was out of the question. She grabbed dishes and a couple of glasses and took everything into the living room. As soon as she cleared the coffee table and laid out the makeshift dinner, the lights blinked off. She walked over to check the switch as Stephen approached carrying a flashlight and two bottles of water.

"I guess the electricity's out again," she said.

He nodded and looked at the spread on the table. "Wow, when did you do all this?"

"While you were busy with the generator. Any luck?"

"Not working. I guess we're gonna have to make do with candles and flashlight until morning." He looked down at the table. "So what do we have here?" he asked.

"Dinner, or rather, everything I could scrounge around in the kitchen and pantry. To tell you the truth, I didn't expect to find this much. I expected everything to have been cleaned out by the management company."

"Management company?" he asked with surprise. He had no idea she'd hired a management company.

"Yes," she replied haltingly, "uh, a friend, an old

friend hired them shortly after Dad died. He took care of everything up until awhile ago. I just found out two days ago that the house is in trouble. It's in foreclosure."

"I know."

"That's why I came down. I'm here to stop it."

"I assumed you didn't want the property," he said.

"I do want it," she said, unable to keep a pleading tone out of her voice. "I had no idea it was in trouble, that the payments weren't being handled. Now I don't know if I can even stop it. They mentioned that there would be an auction. This was my father's sanctuary. I don't want to lose this, too."

"I see," Stephen said, slightly confused. "And this management company was supposed keep up with all the payments?"

"Yes, plus clean out the house, or rather more like keep it livable. You know, mow the yard, pay the water and electric, and secure the windows in case of storms, things like that." He nodded. "Anyway, enough about all that. Come and sit. We should eat."

He opened their water bottles as she divided the mismatched smorgasbord. They ate talking mainly about her father, the house and childhood memories.

"I assume you live close since you know my father— knew my father," Mia said.

"I live fairly close."

"So you're originally from around here?" she asked.

"No, I'm from Miami. My mother's from Key West. My grandfather is the sheriff," he said.

She nodded. "So you went into the family business, huh?"

"You could say that," he said guardedly. Then he changed the conversation quickly, averting the topic of his family business. He wasn't ready for Mia to know about his family. He needed time. "This was good," he remarked on the meal they'd shared.

She smiled. "Not exactly nine courses at the Savoy."

"Maybe not, but tonight it tasted just as good." A moment of stillness paused between them as they listened to the wind howling outside and the heavy rains pounding on the roof.

"Guess I'd better take care of these," she said, standing to clear the dishes.

"Let me help," he said, preparing to stand.

"No, sit. It's not a lot to do. I'll be right back."

Stephen nodded, deciding to let her go. He needed the time to clear his mind. He sat back looking around the familiar house. It was exactly the same, but for some reason Leo's home felt different with Mia there. It was like she'd been missing all along.

Looking at her was killing him, but then again, not looking at her was eating him alive. She had showered and changed into a summer dress with only two straps holding it in place. He closed his eyes and pictured it. The fit curved perfectly to her tight body as if it were made for her. Her back was exposed, and all he kept thinking about was touching her.

Then of course, the low dip in front was driving him to madness. Her breasts tipped and teased just enough to excite his imagination. The taste earlier just wasn't enough. He wanted more. She was killing him, but the heavenly demise was oh-so-worth it.

With no electricity for a blow-dryer, her hair was still damp and pulled back, trailing over her shoulders and down her back. And every time she got close he felt his body harden. Even now his body ached to be with her.

He opened his eyes and looked around. She was still in the kitchen and he needed to refocus his thoughts. He saw a suitcase still sitting at the base of the stairs.

"I'll take your other suitcase upstairs," he said as he grabbed it up and took it to what Leo had once told him was her room. The door was open, so he walked in. The other suitcase was open on the chair with clothes pouring out. She'd obviously been in a hurry to dress. He set the suitcase carried beside the chair then looked around. The room belonged to a little girl with its dolls and pillows fluffed on the bed.

As he passed the dresser to leave he saw an interesting book. He picked it up and read the title. Smiling, he browsed through it and lost himself in the text.

When Mia walked in and saw him, she stopped short.

"Interesting reading?" he asked her, holding the book up to her. He read the title with a huge smile on his face. *"How to Lose Control in the Bedroom and Get What You Want."*

She reached for it. "It was a gift," she said, fighting the flush that swarmed her cheeks. She was completely mortified.

"From a lover?" he asked.

"No, from my sister, my stepsister. It was a joke, a gag gift for my birthday."

"Ah," he said, "a gag gift, I see."

"Well, actually, I have this issue with letting go, losing control." She sighed. "And I can't believe I just told you that."

"So you think this book will perhaps help you lose control?"

She shrugged. "Something like that."

"You don't need a book for that, Mia." She looked

at him. His implication was clear. "So, have you learned anything interesting so far?" he asked, reaching for the book again. She gave it to him and watched as he flipped to the list of chapters.

"I guess I could ask you the same thing," she said.

"The Art of Seductive Foreplay chapter was pretty interesting, but I have to say I was more intrigued by—" he glanced down at the open book "—Fulfilling Fantasies."

"I hadn't gotten that far yet," she said. "What does the book suggest?"

"A number of interesting possibilities, but the number one suggestion is to fulfill a fantasy of your own."

"Hmm, I see, and how does that work exactly?"

"Mia, we've been dancing around this all night. Maybe it's the storm or maybe it's something more. I don't know," he said, hoping not to make her too nervous. "But I do know that there's obviously something going on between us, an attraction. The question is, what do we do about it?"

"What are our options?" she asked.

"We can explore it or keep our distance and let it pass."

She nodded and slowly walked toward the bed. She picked up a doll and held it gently, protectively. "Stephen, I just had a pretty bad breakup a few months ago. It got ugly and it left me in doubt about my…"

"Abilities to please?" he offered. When she nodded, he said, "Thus, the book, the dress, the kiss. Am I a test subject?"

She half shrugged. "I'm sorry. I guess I was curious to see what another man thought."

"I don't know about this other guy, or other men, but make no mistake—you are a very desirable woman."

"Desirable I can do. It's what happens afterward that

seems to be the problem. I guess I want to control so much that I come off as frigid."

He smiled and chuckled. "I doubt that. If a man thinks of a woman as frigid, then perhaps he isn't doing his job correctly to ensure mutual enjoyment and pleasure in their lovemaking. A selfish lover will often blame the other person for his own shortcomings."

She smiled, relieved. That was exactly what she wanted to hear. In five minutes he made her feel more accepted and aroused than Neal had ever been able to do in three years. "You think so, huh?"

"I know so."

"So you think the book is useless?"

"Oh no, not at all." He flipped through it again. "It does offer other suggestions that might be interesting to try sometimes."

"You know you still didn't answer my question," she said.

"What question was that?"

"Fulfilling fantasies—how does that work?"

"Do you want me to tell you or do you want me to show you?"

"Show me."

Clinically she knew all about dopamine levels and pheromones and that the euphoria of emotions was just a chemical reaction stimulated in the brain. That was all Sex 101, but this was different. She was excited and aroused by just looking at Stephen. Their current conversation was getting her even more excited.

"Come here," he said softly, holding his hand out to her and smiling.

She tossed the doll on the chair. A shiver raced through her as she walked over to him and took his hand. He didn't move until she stood right in front of him. He let go and trailed his hand up her arm, to her shoulder, her neck then to her chin. It traveled along the sweet curve then straight down the front of her. She closed her eyes, feeling the tingling sensation as his hand dipped to the swell of her breasts. She inhaled quickly feeling his finger trace back up to her chin.

"Open your eyes," he whispered.

She did. Her heart pounded in her chest. And with just the slightest tilt upward, they looked into each other's eyes, his dark as sin, hers soft and wanting. The penetrating intensity of his gaze took her breath away. She stood immobile, just staring at him, taking everything in, and feeling her body want him.

"Kiss me," he said.

Then, with the slightest motion, she leaned forward and kissed him. Slow, soft and deliberate they savored the sweet lusciousness of the kiss. Pressure increased then released over and over again, lips to lips, mouth to mouth. Their tongues mated, dancing that slow groove of pleasure. She held tight to his shirt.

"Tell me your fantasies, Mia," he prompted as the raging swell of passion built inside of him. She felt his need press into her. He was already hard. The thought made her shudder and caused her stomach to tremble. The excitement of what she was about to do with a complete stranger made the moment even more tantalizing.

"I don't have any fantasies," she said.

"Then tell me what you like."

She placed her hands on his chest and smiled. Touching him was what she'd wanted to do all evening. "I think I like touching you," she admitted freely, surprising herself.

"Do you?" he asked. "In that case…" He pulled his T-shirt up over his head then tossed it onto the chair.

Mia sighed, admiring her find. His chest was magnificent. He kissed her then and her mind went blank. The man wobbled her brain to mush with his mouth. She couldn't think or reason, let alone direct her brain to take control.

"What else do you want from me, Mia?" he asked.

"Kiss me," she said. She opened her mouth to speak, but his mouth closed hungrily over hers a second time. The kiss swayed her. She rocked against him, feeling her body melt. When the kiss ended, she was breathless.

"What else?"

"I don't know," she whispered.

"Yes, you do, tell me."

She sighed. "I don't know," she repeated.

"Tell me, Mia," he prompted again, "I need to give you this. Tell me your fantasy. Tell me what you want."

"I want you to touch me, pamper me, love me…" she said in a voice that quivered and trailed off.

"I thought you'd never ask," he whispered through a smile.

He took her hand and moved to the bed, then sat, bringing her to stand between his legs. When she reached to touch him, he leaned away. "No, this is your fantasy. I touch you, I pamper you, I love you. Turn around."

She turned slowly, sensing his hands circle her waist. She closed her eyes feeling him reach up and release the perfectly tied bow from around her neck. She felt the dress slacken. Instinctively, she grabbed the scant fabric at her breasts, holding it in place.

Then she felt him slowly pull the zipper down. The dress loosened to her waist. Her back was completely exposed. He stroked the full length of her shoulders, arms and back kissing and caressing the curves while massaging her tenderly. Instinctively, she stiffened.

"Relax," he implored.

She nodded, but she knew she wouldn't, couldn't. Relaxing meant losing control, and losing control meant giving all of herself to someone else. That, she couldn't do.

"You know, this is probably a very bad idea," she said nervously, still holding the scant fabric to her breasts. He licked the small of her back. She gasped but he held her closer. "And we're probably gonna regret this one of these days. But right now…" She moaned as he licked her again. "But right now, I just want to…" She gasped as he bit then kissed her right hip. Her mind went blank and her hands fell to her sides.

He licked the center of her back as his hands moved to the front and cupped her breasts. Her stomach quivered as she looked down and saw his hands on her, covering her. She watched as he tweaked each nipple, hardening them instantly. Then, with the palms of his hands, he circled and tantalized each pebble. This lasted for hours, or days, or years, she had no idea. With his mouth on her back and his hands on her front, she was in erotic ecstasy.

"Turn around," he said. She didn't hear him. She didn't hear anything. The storm winds, the driving rain, the flying debris were all muted. All she heard was the urgent pounding of her heart in her chest and the throbbing pull of need in her stomach. "Turn around," he repeated. She didn't, so he turned her slowly while tugging the dress from her hips.

Her hazy thoughts cleared as she stood before him,

naked except for her lace panties. Suddenly self-conscious, she closed her eyes.

"Look at me, Mia," he said. "Open your eyes."

When she didn't, he placed his hands on her hips and drew her closer, till he leaned in to capture her nipple in his mouth. Suckling gently, he savored each fleshly pull. Grasping the other breast, he encircled them both, kissing, licking and suckling each.

Her eyes opened wide. The sight of his mouth and tongue devouring her weakened her knees. She reeled, but Stephen held her securely continuing his onslaught. Her body felt saturated. She pressed her thighs together.

"No, don't," he said, knowing what she was doing. "I want you wet for me." He ran his hand down the front of her body to the elastic band of her panties, then lower. He caressed her core through the lace. She rose up on her toes and her legs parted of their own volition. "Yes, feel me," he muttered. She nodded, breathing harder, gasping, until she staggered and leaned into him.

He captured her mouth, kissing her fully. His tongue entered, darting in and out playfully. Then his mouth found the sweet spot on her neck. She arched back, giving him what he wanted. Seconds later he captured a pert nipple in his mouth again, and his tongue licked her then he sucked. He was merciless. Her body quivered, her stomach shuddered and every nerve ending tingled. Breathlessly she melted onto him. He held her there an instant before he slowly rolled her onto the bed beside him.

He placed her hands above her head then caressed the length of her body. She moved her hands to her sides and closed her eyes, surrendering to the pleasure he gave her. But he took her hands back up over her head, holding them there with one of his own, while the other rained over the flat of her stomach then stroked upward to encircle one breast at a time. Leisurely, his fingers danced over the tips of her nipples. Moaning, she bit her lower lip, wanting more. Her body was on fire with a sensuous blaze of desire she'd never felt before. The pleasure-pain of his masterful hands was beyond belief.

Her body throbbed, spilling its sweet essence for him. His mouth came to her breast as his hand dipped to her needful hunger. He slipped beneath the lace and she gasped. He parted her sweetness, finding his treasure. Then slowly, gently, he stroked her swollen nub while thrusting his finger deep into her. The fitful rapture intensified and she cried aloud. But that only seemed to increase his persistence. She writhed and squirmed against the mastery of his skill. "I can't," she said, fighting for control.

"Yes, you can, Mia. Let go. Let me touch you. Let me love you."

She opened her mouth to speak just as he intensified his strokes. She gasped, breathless, feeling a wave, a tsunami, a maelstrom coming. "Stephen," she cried out. She opened her eyes then, suddenly aware of everything around her—the storm still raging outside, the soft pillows on the bed beneath her, the feel of his body so close, his hand, his mouth, his fingers.

He pushed her further into the blinding sultry storm. She panted, whimpering as her heart thundered. She shrieked, completely enthralled in the rapture and abandoning all pretense of control. "Stephen," she called again an instant before a quake gripped her, shook her to her core. She screamed again and again as he helped himself to her pleasure.

Moments later she lay curled against his body, half-asleep but fully satiated.

"Why didn't you…"

But he silenced her. "Later. Sleep now." He held her protectively close as the winds and rain lulled her slowly to sleep.

Chapter 9

Stephen jerked awake when he heard something. With sharpened instincts, he sat up quickly and looked around. The room was still dark except for a dimmed lanternlike flashlight on the side table. He glanced at his watch. It was early morning. He listened again. There was the low rumble of thunder with a steady pounding of rain and the constant whirl of wind, but there was something else, a knocking noise. He listened close. There it was again, a low banging sound. He glanced down at Mia still asleep beside him. He eased up and off the bed, took the flashlight then went downstairs and looked around.

Everything was fine. He checked the windows and doors then tried his walkie-talkie, but didn't get a signal. The storm was still causing interference. He was just about to go back upstairs when he heard the noise again.

It was coming from out front. He grabbed his raincoat and opened the front door. The weather was just as bad as it has been earlier. Wind whipped at him and rain peppered his face the second he stepped outside. He looked around. Nothing seemed out of place, considering just about everything was out of place. Then he heard it again, a banging, louder this time. He moved to the side of Mia's car and saw that a section of picket fence had uprooted and was hitting against the car door. He grabbed the fence and secured it to the side. After one last look around he headed back inside.

He dried off in the mudroom then debated going back upstairs. As he considered it, he went back into the living room and sat down. It seemed strange being in Leo's house now. He'd slept here before, many times, when Leo came home from the hospital, when treatments didn't go well, and even when they did. That was before, and never in her room. Until last night.

"Stephen, are you down there?"

At the sound of Mia's voice, he looked up. "Yeah, in the living room."

Mia came downstairs and stood at the base of the steps. He noticed that she was wearing his police-issue T-shirt. "Are you okay?" she asked.

"Yeah, just checking out a noise," he said.

She looked around. "What kind of noise?" she asked, moving across the room toward him.

"A fence panel was knocking against the car door. You might want to check damages in the morning."

"I guess I'll be lucky if that's the worst that happens." She looked around awkwardly, like she wanted to say something but was stalling. "So, how is it out there?"

"The same," he said. Then he smiled. "Nice shirt."

"I kind of like it, too, but you can have it back when you want."

"What if I want it now?" he challenged.

"Now?" she asked. He nodded slowly and waited patiently.

She looked into his eyes. In the muted darkness she realized he was challenging her. She smiled and took a step back. "If you want it now, you'll have to come up and get it." She took another step back.

"Wait. I don't have any condoms," he said.

"I do. Dozens." She turned then went upstairs hoping he'd follow.

Stephen joined her in the bedroom almost immediately, and she smiled at his promptness. He walked over to her as she knelt on the edge of the bed, her hands behind her back.

"What do you have?" he asked. She showed him a box of condoms then dumped them on the bed. He laughed and nodded as she smiled. She was definitely prepared. He chuckled again. "Should I even ask?"

"It was part of my birthday gift."

"From your stepsister again?" When she nodded, he chuckled and shook his head. "She must be a very—"

"Oh yeah, she most definitely is," she agreed.

When he stood in front of her she grabbed the hem of the T-shirt and slowly, seductively pulled it up over her head. She was completely naked. He smiled and licked his lips at seeing her, obviously enjoying the view. "You like?" she asked timidly.

"No, not yet," he said, then reached out and ran his finger around her breast causing the nipple to tighten instantly. She shivered. Smiling at his quick handiwork, he repeated the action on the other breast. He didn't speak at first. He just stood there smiling and nodding. Her nipples seemed to get even harder under his intense stare. "Now I like."

She opened her mouth to respond, but he immediately encircled her waist and drew her flush to his body. He kissed her and her mind went to mush as she moaned the pleasure of her consent. Swept up in the power of his merciless passion, she eagerly surrendered her body, melting to his. He sucked her tongue, delving deep, then licked and tickled the roof of her mouth. The kiss was exquisite. Nothing like she'd ever experienced before. She squirmed and writhed against his deep penetration increasing an even greater lustful hunger with each movement. She tried to give as good as she got, but he was too masterful and she was just too impatient.

She was breathless when the kiss ended. And all she wanted was him back in her mouth again. But he didn't oblige, not right away. Instead he showered her with tiny kisses from her mouth to her ear, then down her neck and over her shoulder. She nearly shattered into pieces before arching back. She called out his name but he instantly silenced her with his mouth on hers in a mind-blowing kiss that was off the scale.

He devoured her, once again penetrating her mouth as his hands played havoc with her senses. He kneaded and caressed her breasts then reached back to fondle her rear, playfully massaging her ample ripeness, pressing her ever closer to his hardness. He held her closer, going deeper and deeper. When he released her mouth he dipped to suckle her breasts. She arched back giving him all he wanted and more.

He pulled the hardened nipple into his mouth, kissed

and licked them mercilessly. She gasped and moaned, barely mindful of anything other than his mouth on her body. He parted her legs, her knees buckled, but he held her so tight she didn't even notice. He began touching her, caressing her, stroking her. She held tight to his shoulders, rocking her hips to his rhythm. The sweet, sensual madness had begun, but this time she wanted more. She wanted all of him. "No," she gasped, "I want you inside me this time."

"Paciencia, mi amor," he said. *"Paciencia."*

Breathlessly she called out his name as passion pushed her closer to the pinnacle of ecstasy. She grabbed his shoulders, holding tight, feeling the swell of abandoned rapture surge through her. "Now, Stephen," she gasped. But he continued kissing and licking her breast and his hand prodded her further, stroking her. "Stephen, I want you inside me."

Her hand slid down his shoulder to the elastic waistband of his briefs. "Take these off," she requested. He did, instantly freeing his erection. She looked down at him. He was much bigger and longer than she anticipated. "Lay back," she said. When he did, she grabbed a condom off the bed then sat on top of him, straddling his naked body. She smiled down at him as she opened the package and protected them both in one smooth motion. Then she rose up and impaled herself onto his steel erection. His length and thickness made her gasp. She closed her eyes tight, sitting still and enjoying the slow, sweet burn of her body surrounding his. He filled her completely and she loved it.

Then she began to move, riding his body slow and easy at first, like an undulating wave. She gelled and rolled, rocked and pitched, swaying her hips after each plunge. His shaft throbbed and swelled fuller, tightening each time she mounted and released him. She raised her hands above her head quickening the pace, and his hands covered her breasts and his fingers tweaked her nipples. She quivered as her hips continued to gyrate. She gorged her fill with even more of him over and over again.

Then in progression the cadence slowly increased. Her breathing halted as she gasped for air. A scream, buried deep, threatened to release, but still she moved faster. The accelerated friction of her body grinding his sent wave after wave of torrid tremors into her. She quivered and quaked and kept going, faster and faster, in and out, rocking her hips to her rhythm.

Her heart beat wildly and her breathing was erratic. This was too much. She expected to pass out in the next few seconds. But she didn't. She just kept rocking her hips, grinding his body, faster and faster. Her head spun; she was losing her balance. She leaned over grabbing his shoulders to steady herself. He held her hips and then reached up to capture a nipple in his mouth. The unexpected delight made her shriek. He suckled hard, licked and lavished all manner of pleasure-pain to her nipple and breast. She called out his name, still rocking, riding him, on and off, in and out, faster and faster.

Abandoning all restraint, she felt a fierce hunger as each thrusting motion drew moans and gasps of rapturous pleasure from her. She surged closer and closer to the edge, then with one last deep plunge she tipped over. Her climax was blinding. She screamed, digging her nails deep into his skin. Seconds later she screamed again as he followed, calling her name and spilling the abundance of his force into her. He went stiff, yet his erection was still firm. He rocked his hips, hitting the tiny, throbbing bud again, making her scream once more. He obviously liked the way she bit her nails into his skin because he made her scream again and again. Each time he arched his hips she climaxed. Shuddering and shaking, quivering breathlessly, she barely gasped, "Enough." He stilled, letting her be. She collapsed and lay on top of him, drained and completely spent.

"Paciencia, mi amor," he said. "We're not done yet."

Still breathless, Mia smiled, intrigued by his statement. Her mind was hazy, swimming wildly in the afterglow of his skills. No book ever warned her about this, about him. She couldn't imagine what he was talking about, but she soon found out.

He lay her beside him and began touching her, massaging her body from top to bottom. *"Esta, mi amor, es mi fantasía,"* he whispered.

Mia didn't respond. She knew the words, "this, my love, is my fantasy." But, she was too far gone to think about what he'd said. Her body had been cherished, loved and devoured. She'd lost control and loved it. By the time he'd finished touching her she was ready for more. With him on the bottom and her on top again, they danced the horizontal dance of love once more.

An hour later, Stephen looked at the woman sleeping in the bed beside him. Their naked bodies were intertwined as her legs wrapped leisurely over and between his. He wasn't dreaming. Mia was really here and they'd just made love. He looked down at his sleeping beauty. This was the woman he'd been fixated on for the last several months. She was as beautiful as he'd fantasized, his dream come to life. How could he have fallen even more in love with her?

Leo had talked about her nonstop, about her childhood living with her overprotective grandmother, her time with her mother drifting from stepfather to stepfather. But the times she stayed with him here in Key West were his favorite conversations. They talked for hours about their father-daughter fishing trips, boating, sailing, even walks on the beach. They shopped, picnicked, played ball, laughed and talked.

At first Stephen was slightly envious of Mia. She had done things with Leo that he would have loved to have done. Things his own father had never taken the time to do with him. Carlos Morales was always too busy. He was obsessed with power and success. Having grown up wealthy, he pushed to remain on top. This required him to work long and hard, and like his struggling father before, he never had time for family. He still didn't. In the end, it was his loss. And it was Stephen's friendship with Leo that had evolved into Stephen's only father-son relationship.

They went fishing, hung out at the local sporting events and did exactly what he intended to do with his sons and daughters. Stephen smiled, looking down on the woman that would bear his children. Of course she had no idea how he felt. He couldn't risk scaring her. So as much as he wanted to tell her how much he loved her, he held back and showed her instead.

She hummed and snuggled closer to his body. He looked down the length of her perfectly naked form. His arousal returned instantly. She was everything he ever wanted and now she was here. In time he hoped to make her his. He reached out and gently stroked her face.

She awoke smiling. "Hmm, hey," she purred dreamily.

"Hey yourself," he said, smiling at her.

"What were you doing?"

"Watching you sleep."

"Funny, you don't look like a crazed psychopath."

He laughed heartily. "Don't worry, I'm not. I was just remembering some of the things Leo and I talked about."

"Like what?" she asked.

"You."

She shook her head. "See, that's so odd that the two of you were friends. My dad didn't have a lot of friends. He always found a way to alienate them."

"Oh, he tried with me, too. We had our massive blowout, but eventually he and I came to an understanding."

"What was the blowout about?" she asked.

"Family and fathers," he said.

"Fathers?" she asked, then sat up slightly. "Are you a father?"

He smiled. "No, not yet."

She nodded thankfully, hoping she didn't look as relieved as she felt. For reasons she wasn't ready to analyze, she didn't want to think about Stephen's other life just yet. She wanted him all to herself. If there was a woman somewhere in the background, that's where she wanted her to stay, at least for tonight. "But you want to be a father, right?"

"Yes, I think I'd like ten, maybe fifteen kids."

Mia laughed. "Are you insane? What woman is going to have ten or fifteen kids?"

"Perhaps you," he said too seriously. Mia looked at him oddly. He stilled, hoping he hadn't scared her. By the expression on her face, he had. He quickly regrouped. "I'm joking," he said playfully, smiling and hoping she'd relax again. Mia smiled. When her expression changed, he relaxed. "Okay, ten or fifteen kids might be a bit much. Maybe I'll compromise."

"I think that's wise," she said easily.

"Do you want children and how many?" he asked her.

"Uh, to tell you the truth I haven't really thought about it lately. Before, like you, I wanted like a dozen kids. I was an only child, except for my stepsisters, so I wanted a huge family. Then I got engaged a few years back. Don't ask, it didn't end well. Anyway, now I don't know if I want any."

"I hope you change your mind. You'd be a wonderful mother."

"You think so?" she asked.

"Definitely," he said.

"You're nothing like him, you know. My dad."

"Actually, I'm more like Leo than you'd think."

"If that's the case, then that would make you arrogant and egotistical. That's how my mom always described my dad. She said that was the reason she married him. She fell in love with his talent and bravado. Then she realized that the man and the bravado were easier to live with than the man and the talent. He was too good for his own good." She shook her head. "That doesn't sound like you."

"But you don't really know me, do you?"

"No, I suppose I don't, not really." Then, considering the circumstance, she added, "I can't believe I'm lying in bed with a complete stranger."

He reached down and plucked her nipple. "I wouldn't exactly say we were complete strangers. We did just make love. And…" He leaned down capturing her mouth and kissed her possessively.

Mia's body ignited and her mind whirled in a million different directions. To hell with rational thinking. This was lust, pure and simple. And right now, for once in her perfectly processed and controlled life, she intended to step up and take something for herself. She smiled, feeling the firm strength of Stephen's chest as he rolled on top of her. He was already hard and she was wet and ready. She looked down at his bold erection and smiled. This was for her.

"Do you remember chapter seventeen?" he asked. She shook her head and reached for the book. She found the page, looked at him and smiled, anticipating the time of her life.

He leaned up and took his time looking down her body. She smiled and spread her legs for him. His hand stroked her breasts then her stomach, ending between her legs. She gasped and bit her lower lip. This man was too intense. In turn she touched his mouth then scratched her nails down his neck to his chest then as low as she could reach, pressing harder and harder as she went. She knew she'd leave a mark. But she wanted possession this time and he understood.

An instant later he grabbed a condom and covered himself. She grabbed his buttocks and pulled him down hard onto her body. He thrust into her and she shrieked with blinding delight. This was what she wanted, intensity and power. The fierceness of her insatiable hunger for him drove her to rapturous anticipation. He surged and she met each thrust with equal fervor. Unrestrained and with abandoned vigor she sought the darker side of her passion. Shelved was the tender, sensual lovemaker. This time she wanted him too much for that.

Thrust after thrust they plowed and plunged deeper

and deeper, penetrating their lustful passion for release. Then as the wave approached she delighted as it came fast and furious taking them at the same time. In pushup form he held still and she whipped her hips higher and higher, meeting his body in midair. She maneuvered just right to catch her swollen nub as she welcomed his engorged shaft. She wrapped her arms around his neck, lifting her body off the bed and letting the power of his arms and legs seal them together. She screamed his name and he called out to her. He held firm and she shuddered and quaked. The pinnacle, the orgasm, the climax, the mind-mangling come arrived in all its ravenous rage. And it was better than anything she had ever experienced.

Spent and quivering, Stephen eased his body down onto her then beside her, rolling over and holding her close. A fear had gripped him. He wanted her so much that perhaps his blinding passion had been too powerful. "Mia, talk to me. Are you okay?"

"I have never been more okay in my life," she rasped, still breathless. She snuggled closer and formed her body to the now familiar position. They fell asleep almost immediately. And all she could think about was the next time.

Chapter 10

Morning came, but it wasn't the happy shining brightness she remembered so well from her childhood visits to Key West. On the contrary, the weather was still bad, but perhaps not as bad as the night before. Or maybe it just seemed better having Stephen there with her. The winds seemed to have died down for now and the torrential rain had slackened to a perpetually steady downpour. Lying still, Mia listened as the wind gusts trembled the shingles on the roof and rocked the tree branches into the side of the house. The sounds were ominous, although again, not nearly as bad as it was the night before.

It was going to be one of those days. She could feel it. Just like yesterday when everything seemed to go wrong—the drive down in the horrific weather, the courthouse closing early. Only Stephen had been the exception to the day's insanity. She smiled as her body seemed to ease deeper into the cushion of the mattress just by thinking about him. Her thoughts drifted back to their time together.

The man was insatiable. His appetite for bringing her to climax was ravenous. She came so many times she'd lost count. Sleepily she reached out hoping to find him still beside her, but she knew he wouldn't be. He had kissed her and whispered earlier that he needed to get to work. She vividly remembered him touching and stroking her breast to awaken her, then his naked body pressed intimately behind hers. He was already erect and she was already wet for him. They'd made love then he kissed her and slipped away.

Mia smiled and stretched, opening her eyes. She lazily looked around her childhood bedroom. The first thing she saw was the book lying open on the nightstand. The next thing she realized was that she was still naked. She smiled, remembering all of chapter twelve. They'd proved it could be done, twice.

She got up slowly and wrapped the sheet around her stiff body. Last night she'd used muscles she didn't even know she had. *Damn, that man was amazing.* She shivered just thinking about chapter seventeen. Smiling a silly grin, she kicked the sheet behind her. She should really be embarrassed, but for some reason she just couldn't muster the emotion. Last night was phenomenal. Stephen was phenomenal. She had no idea sex could be so incredible. She wasn't a virgin, but she might as well have been before last night.

She checked her cell phone on the dresser; it had no signal. Then she toggled the light switch. Still no electricity. Afterward she went into the kitchen and found a bag with a folded paper attached. She opened and read the note aloud. "'I thought you might need sustenance after last night. I'll see you later, Stephen.'" She chuckled and looked into the bag. There was a cup of hot tea, a wrapped pastry, orange juice and water. She pulled out and prepared her tea then opened her pastry and took a bite. The warm chewy delight was filled with a quichelike mixture. She ate half and drank her juice before even sitting down.

After breakfast she washed up, changed clothes and straightened up her bedroom. If Stephen was coming back as he'd mentioned, she didn't want the place to be a complete mess.

Outside it was still raining, but the wind gusts didn't seem as severe. She hoped that the hurricane might be winding down. It seemed a perfect time to go outside and assess the storm's damage.

With her father's rain slicker and galoshes on, Mia walked around outside checking the windows and shutters. She noticed for the first time just how badly the house had been neglected. She began picking up fallen branches and debris. A long section of fence had been torn away, so she gathered the pieces together and put them in what was left of the shed.

She gathered more debris and stored it away with plans to call a removal company in the next few days. While gathering in the front yard she found a Foreclosure–For Immediate Auction sign. Her heart sank. She didn't realize it had been put up. She took it to the shed and tossed it in.

After about an hour cleaning up Mia, completely drenched again, went back inside. As soon as she closed the door she heard her cell phone ring. The fickle signal, apparently, was back. She ran upstairs to get it.

"Mia, where are you? I've been trying to call you all day."

"Hi, Mom," she said dryly.

"Where on earth are you? This connection is horrible."

Mia paused a moment before answering. She knew her mother would have a hysterical fit when she found out what she was doing. That's why she didn't tell her before she left.

Katherine James Truman Kent was considered by all to be a woman of power, standing and means. She had married well three times. Once for prestige with her father, Leo. Once for money with Janelle's father and lastly with Nya's father for connections. Now she finally had everything she wanted.

"I'm at Dad's place."

"In Key West? Are you out of your mind? The weather report said that there's a hurricane down there. I thought you were going to Paradise Island with Janelle and Nya."

"No, I had to change my plans. I need to save Dad's house."

"So you risked your life to save an old shack. If this isn't the silliest thing you've done yet. Mia, get in your car and get back here."

"Mom, I'm a bit old for chastising. I need to do this."

"Why?"

"Because I just do," she said, not wanting to go into detail about her feelings with her mother, the queen of cold.

"Mia, I spoke with Neal's mother. She told me that Neal has been asking for you."

Mia rolled her eyes. "I don't want to hear this."

"Mia, the man made a mistake. Surely you can see that."

"Mom, a mistake is forgetting to pay your electric bill. He lied to me about everything. How can you possibly be on his side after everything he put me through?"

"I'm not on his side, Mia. I just want you to be happy."

"My fiancé eloped with a coed. How could that make me happy? I was humiliated via the World Wide Web. All of my friends, my colleagues…" She stopped not wanting to even think about it. "Mom, I have to go. I need to change and get to the county court building. It was closed yesterday, but hopefully it's open now."

"I don't know why you're going through all this. Just let the bank sell the house and be done with it."

"I can't. Its Dad's house. He left it to me to take care of. I let him down the last two years of his life, I can't let him down again."

"Mia, you didn't let him down."

"I could have been here when he died, but I wasn't. I was too stubborn, too angry, when he called. He needed me and I didn't come to him. He told me to get rid of Neal and I didn't listen."

"That's an old argument, Mia. Your father's gone and I really think Neal's changed."

"I can't get into that with you right now, Mom. I need to get to town."

"This really doesn't sound like a good idea."

"Good idea or not, it's what I need to do."

"Fine, just be careful out there. Call me tonight."

"My cell's been going out. If you don't hear from me, the connections are just down again."

Mia closed her cell and checked the battery level. It was low. She couldn't plug it in since there was no electricity. She wanted to preserve the battery for when she needed to make an outgoing call, so she dropped it into her pocketbook to hopefully charge in town.

Outside the sky was still dark and overcast, but the winds had calmed down to a brisk warm breeze and the rain slacked to a steady heavy drizzle. Maybe the worst was over, Mia considered as she turned on the radio hoping to get more information.

To her surprise the Holy Terror was still on the air. Apparently hurricane advisories were still being issued and he warned not to be lulled by the break in weather.

"Local officials expect flooding and severe weather, and remind residents that this is still a dangerous storm."

Driving into town, Mia saw firsthand the damage Hurricane Ana had done. What looked like a ghost town the day before looked more like a war zone today.

As she drove she noticed only a few cars on the road. She assumed most people were still away. She pulled into the same spot she had the day before, got out and walked up to the building. Before she even got there she saw that the office was closed. Frustrated, she went back to her car. She had two choices—go back to Atlanta and forget about the whole thing or stay and wait for the office to open no matter how long it took. She decided to wait.

But waiting meant she needed to get supplies in the house. She looked around at the closed stores on the street. There had to be someplace in town to get supplies. Driving around, she noticed an open grocery store. An hour later she came out with four grocery bags and even found the local *Key West Citizen* newspaper.

Her next stop was to a hardware store. The shelves

were mostly empty and the store ran on a generator that blinked the lights every ten minutes, but she picked up what she needed to sustain her for a few days or at least until the county office opened again. She loaded the supplies into the trunk of the car and noticed that the winds had picked up again. The sky seemed darker as if there'd be a downpour any minute. She needed to make one last stop.

Mia remembered seeing a coffee shop open as she drove into town. It was just down the block and around the corner. They touted free Wi-Fi, so she hoped there was electricity that she might recharge her cell phone. As she walked to the small shop the weather was steadily getting worse. The wind began gusting and what had been a light mist turned to drizzle. She quickened her pace hoping to get back to her dad's house before it got worse.

She turned the corner and saw Stephen standing in front of the coffee shop beneath a stationary awning talking to two other officers. She smiled instantly. He was too handsome and the thought of her taking him out of that uniform gave her a brand-new fantasy to consider. Seconds later her smile slowly faded when the female officer turned and Stephen wrapped his arms around her playfully. He smiled and laughed then reached out and touched her swollen stomach. It protruded at least six months.

Mia's heart sank instantly. She had asked Stephen and he'd denied being married or engaged. She hadn't pursued other committed relations.

Of course they didn't have any connection other than the one night they'd spent together, so her being jealous was ridiculous. Still, she could feel the pain in her heart deepen. Surprisingly she didn't have this reaction when she found out about Neal. She'd felt humiliated, but never jealous.

It was one night, she reminded herself. One night with a stranger, nothing more, nothing less. She had enjoyed being with him, not just sexually, although that was incredible, too, but she also just liked talking with him. He listened and seemed to care and understand. Maybe it was all a show to get her into bed. But she'd wanted and pursued him, not the other way around.

Without realizing it, Mia had stopped walking. She stood across the street watching him as he interacted with the female officer with a familiarity she'd never know. Sadness filled her. As apropos to her mood, thunder rumbled in the distance. She started walking. By the time she got to the coffee shop, Stephen and the other officer had walked off and another woman, a civilian, walked up. Mia approached the shop's door. She smiled at the two women talking. "Good morning," she said.

"Good morning," both women said, turning to face her.

"See, Helen, another brave soul out in this mess."

"Well, Natalia, this soul is getting out of this craziness and heading to my brother's place. I'm already packed to go, but wouldn't you know, I'd have a taste for your sister's key lime pie, of all things? You ladies have a good day, and be safe. Natalia, I'll see you in a few days."

Mia smiled and nodded as the woman hurried away. The officer Stephen had hugged stayed. "So, what brings you out in this craziness?" she asked Mia.

"Hunger and bare cupboards. Is the coffee shop still open?" Mia asked.

"Yes, sure, but better hurry if you want baked goods. They go fast when the weather's clear. When it's like this you can just about forget it."

Mia smiled at the woman's friendly remark. She seemed likeable even though Mia really didn't want to like her. "Do you live around here?"

"Yes, not too far. Are you lost?"

"No, actually I was just wondering if you might know when the county clerk's office might be open again."

"Probably not for a couple more days, that's if the storm passes," the woman said. "But actually the woman who just left, Helen Parker, works there. Shame you didn't ask earlier. She might have opened the office for you."

Mia turned. The other woman, Helen Parker, had already gotten into her car and driven away. "Oh no," she said miserably. "Helen Parker, that's who I needed to see."

"Is there a problem?" Natalia asked.

"No, well, actually yes. I need to speak with Ms. Parker. It's extremely important. Do you know where she lives or how to get in touch with her?"

"Yes, I know where she lives, but as you heard, she's going to her brother's place."

"Do you know where he lives?" Mia asked.

Natalia half smiled, amazed at Mia's adamant persistence. "Helen has six brothers scattered across Florida."

Mia was instantly dejected. She nodded. "I see, thanks anyway."

"I'm sure the office will be open again in a couple of days. Are you visiting Key West?"

"Not really. I used to vacation here a while ago. My dad lived here most of his life. His name was Leo James."

"Leo, sure, everybody knew Leo. I'm sorry for your loss."

"You knew my father?"

"Sure, Key West is actually a very small community in the off season. After a while everyone knows everyone. Leo was a really nice man. He'll be greatly missed."

"Thank you. It's nice of you to say. He was difficult."

"He was real."

"You're right," Mia said, finding herself enjoying the conversation and liking the woman's friendly personality. "I'm Mia James."

"Hi, Mia, I'm Natalia Coles. Nice to meet you."

"Likewise, I love your name. It's different."

"Thanks, for some reason our mom and dad gave us all Russian names. Try getting through elementary school with names like Natalia, Dominik, Mikhail, Nikita and Tatiana." They laughed heartily. "So, Mia, when did you get here?"

"Yesterday."

"During the hurricane?" she asked. "Girl, you must have been either desperate to get here or to get away from wherever you were."

Mia looked at her, slightly surprised. Natalia's intuitive perception was amazing. "A little bit of both actually. You're very intuitive."

"Comes with the job," Natalia said, winking.

"Mia."

At the sound of Stephen's voice, Mia turned to him.

"Hi, Sheriff, nice to see you again," she said, trying to be as cool and detached as Neal always told her she was.

"Oh, you two know each other," Natalia surmised. "Mia, we're just about to grab something to eat, why don't you join us?"

"No thanks, I need to get back to the house. The weather looks like it's just about to turn again."

Natalia nodded. "We're still under a hurricane watch."

"Right, so I guess I really need to get back. It was nice meeting you, Natalia. Take care, Sheriff." She quickly turned and walked away, swallowing hard and taking a deep breath. So what if she didn't have phone access again tonight? There was no way she was going to sit and have lunch with Stephen and his "friend."

"Mia," Stephen called out, hurrying to catch up with her.

Mia kept walking as he fell in step beside her. "She's nice. I like her. Baby momma?" she asked.

Stephen turned to look back at Natalia. "She's my cousin and you're right, she is nice. You two would really get along."

"Look, Stephen, don't stress it. It's all good. I know the science and psychology of what happened between us last night. We both needed a physical release to counteract the strong emotions caused by the hurricane."

"That's a bit clinical, don't you think? Is that all you think happened between us last night?" he asked.

"We were—" She paused and corrected herself. "We are strangers. Last night was last night. The opportunity presented itself and we went with it. No harm, no foul, right?"

"Wrong. Mia—"

"You'd better get back. Natalia's probably waiting for you," she said. "I gotta go."

Stephen glanced over his shoulder, seeing Natalia standing outside the restaurant smiling at him. "We need to talk, Mia. I'll be by later."

"Why? What's there to talk about?"

"We need to talk," he said again. "There are things you should know. Things you need to know."

She shook her head. "Stephen, there's nothing to say."

"Mia, believe me, there is," he said as he walked her back to the car.

"Stephen, last night was really special and I don't want it to turn into something awkward between us. I don't know your situation or how long I'll be here, but I'd like to have you as a friend or maybe—" She stopped, catching herself.

"Or maybe what?" he asked.

"Nothing," she said, walking as quickly as she could. She couldn't believe she left it hanging like that.

"I'll come by when I get off," he said.

"No, don't." She unlocked the car door as the rain came down heavier.

"I have to," he said earnestly.

She got in her car and Stephen waited until she drove away. There was so much he wanted to say to her, but the time was never right. He hurried back to the coffee shop, where Natalia was already inside sitting at a table. She was smiling as usual.

"Does she know about you yet?" she asked.

"No, not yet," Stephen said as he sat down. "Not everything."

"For a brilliant businessman, you're obviously clueless."

"I know what I'm doing, Natalia."

She smirked. "Ah yes, the famous last words from every person about to screw up what could have been a good thing."

Stephen frowned. "Do you ever mind your own business?"

"You know I don't, so why even ask?" she said, standing. "I'll be back. I need to talk to Nikita."

Stephen chuckled, totally agreeing with Natalia's statement. She was impossible. As he laughed he looked up seeing his two cousins walk in. Greeting each other, Dominik and Mikhail shook Stephen's hand before they sat. "I didn't know you guys were coming. When did you get back in town?" Stephen asked Mikhail.

"I got in earlier this morning. I figured I'd check out the pier and assess the damage."

"How's it look out there?" Dominik asked.

"Not too bad. Looks like Ana was kinder than the last few storms passing through this way. Most of the larger vessels left days ago and the smaller ones were able to be moored inland."

"So how's it going at the hospital?" Stephen asked Dominik.

"A lot better than we anticipated. We just had a few minor problems, and of course baby Ana arrived last night. Thankfully the city is almost empty, and so there haven't been a lot of injuries."

"So what's going on with you?" Mikhail asked Stephen.

"It's been quiet. As you said, most people left the island, so law enforcement has been light. Plus, I'm still technically on injured reserve, so they only call when I'm needed or for light duty."

"That's not what I mean," Mikhail said. "What's going with you personally? I hear you're in a bit of trouble."

"What do you mean?" Stephen asked.

"Natalia told us you needed our help," Dominik said.

"Exactly. So what's up?" Mikhail added with interest.

Stephen shook his head, puzzled. "I'm fine."

Natalia walked up, greeted her older brothers and then sat. They talked a few minutes about the hurricane then her pregnancy. "So, guess who I just met," Natalia said happily. Stephen looked at her murderously, but she smiled and continued anyway. "I met Leo James's daughter, Mia. She's in town, came in yesterday. She already met our cousin here."

All eyes turned to Stephen. This was the last thing he needed, his family on his case again. As expected, questions and comments followed and a full discussion began.

"Man, of all the women in the world to fall for," Mikhail said, shaking his head in profound astonishment.

"I'm still stunned that you and Leo ever became friends," Dominik added. "What were you thinking when you moved here? You had to know your father would be pissed when he found out."

"Don't you know? That's why he moved here," Natalia said smugly, "to piss Carlos off. Don't you just love Freudian slips?"

"Your psychology degrees are going to get you in trouble one of these days, Gnat," Stephen warned sharply, using the childhood nickname he gave her because she was always buzzing about and annoying him. Even now, years later, she was still driving him crazy.

Natalia laughed and enjoyed his discomfort. "Come on, Esteban." She was the only one who ever used his birth name. "You know I'm right. Leo was the father you always wanted. He was everything Carlos isn't. Of course you bonded with him."

"No offense, cousin, your pops is a trip sometimes," Mikhail added. "I can't believe you worked with him as long as you did."

None of this was anything Stephen hadn't already said to himself. They were right, all of them. As hard as it was at admit to himself, he'd befriended Leo knowing that it would alienate his father even more.

"Come on, let's order. I'm starved," Natalia said.

"You're always starved," Dominik said. "Now more than ever."

"Who's picking up the check?" Mikhail asked.

Dominik shook his head. "Not me. I got it last time."

"You two are ridiculous. I got it this time," Natalia said, more parental than usual. "Just remember, dear brothers and cousin, I have a couple of sons to put through college in a few years, so don't try to break the bank."

Natalia turned to Stephen. "Hey, Esteban, you okay over there?" she asked softly.

"Yeah, just thinking."

"You love Mia." Her voice had softened, became empathetic, even maternal. "You've loved her since before Leo died. To love like that without having ever even met the person is beyond incredible. Leo saw what you were feeling and it was like he was preparing you to be with her. And of course, him asking you to look after her just about sealed it. Take it slow, and remember you know a lot more about her than she knows about you or any of this. There's a good chance she's going to have problems with you because of Carlos. When are you going to tell her everything?"

"I don't know. Soon. I don't have a choice."

"Any indication how she might take it?" she asked.

"What part? That my father intentionally ruined her father's career because of an article that was the truth? That I knew about it and helped? That Leo went back to drinking because of it? That he slowly killed himself by doing everything his doctors told him not to?"

"Carlos used you," she said. "He lied to you."

"It doesn't change the fact that I did it. I went after Leo with everything in my power."

"Then when you found out your father lied to you, you quit."

"Do you really think that's going to matter to her?" he asked sarcastically.

"Maybe, maybe not, but it mattered to Leo. He practically gave you Mia's hand. He told you to watch for her and to take care of her. He had to know she'd be open."

"Whatever was discussed between Leo and me has nothing to do with Mia."

"Oh please, you know it does," Natalia said.

"Whatever. I don't want her to know about any of this, not until I tell her myself."

"Your call," she said, then reached over and squeezed his hand. "Just don't wait too long to tell her. And don't think that her obviously growing feelings for you will dull the pain when she finds out. They won't. She'll just feel betrayed, and believe me, that won't be good."

The waitress arrived and took their orders. Soon lunch arrived and as they ate, the cousins talked, enjoying their family bond. Stephen, however, only half listened. His thoughts were flowing in one direction—Mia.

Chapter 11

Ana was coming back and just like before, she wasn't playing around. Mia drove steadily through the approaching storm, yet her thoughts weren't on the weather or on her driving. Case in point, her car hydroplaned twice. The second time was enough for her to slow down and focus. Still her thoughts wandered.

It wasn't even the fact that the county office was still closed that frustrated her. It was seeing Stephen, a man she knew practically nothing about, with another woman, Natalia. She was pregnant. He said she was his cousin and she believed him, so why was she still so upset?

She didn't even know the man. But the idea, the possibility, of another woman in his life just didn't sit well. It was completely absurd, beyond ridiculous, of course, but there it was. There was no way she was falling for him after just one night together. How was that possible? She was attracted to him, yes, but that was it. It had to be.

But, in those few hours she'd spent with him, she felt more alive and adored than in the last three years with Neal. It wasn't just the sex. It was the closeness they'd shared, the fact that her father liked him and the fact that he made her feel the way she knew she was supposed to feel with a man. She laughed aloud. Ten to fifteen kids? No way. Maybe three or four, but that was it.

Whoa. She gulped, nearly choking on her last breath. The thought came at her from out of the blue. Making love was one thing, but she had just mentally negotiated the number of children they'd have. This can't be right. Nowhere in her books did it mention this part. She never even had that conversation with Neal, the man with whom she was supposedly in love.

"It was the sex," she said aloud. "The mind-blowing, toe-curling orgasms. The man is a masterful genius when it comes to a woman's body. That's why I'm so mixed up and confused." She relaxed back against the seat, satisfied with her conclusion. But somewhere in the back of her mind there was a tiny nagging voice that continued to taunt and question the obvious. How could she fall for a man in a matter of hours?

"Stop it. Stop thinking about him," she ordered herself. "It was one night. Get over it." Forcing herself, Mia focused on the weather, the roads and her driving. Not surprisingly, some of the roads she had easily passed earlier were now completely flooded. She waded through some, detoured and took alternate routes for others, only to be confronted with more flooding and fallen debris. But through it all she drove steadily, hoping a constant pace would get her home. She splashed through deep puddles splitting high water arches along either side of the car. As the puddles got deeper, her anxiety increased.

The wind picked up and the car rocked again, shaking her back to her senses. She steadied it and continued. With certainty, the finality of her previous decision stood. It was attraction, it was lust and that was all. She sighed with relief. She was fine. She was just tired and bemused by the storm and all that went along with it. That included Stephen and their night together. The car pitched to the side, doing a lateral move. Mia held tight, and just like on ice, she let the wheel take her until she could regain control.

Control. That's what she needed, to regain control of her life. Just like before, right after Neal eloped with his coed and their personal intimate life went public. She had felt sorry for herself, she'd mourned their relationship then went into a blue funk, but after long exhausting conversations with Janelle and Nya and especially herself, she'd come out better than ever. Stronger, and more determined to get her life back, just as her father had always taught her. Never give up on yourself.

"Just a few more blocks," she said, patting the steering wheel affectionately. She looked ahead seeing a puddle that was definitely too deep to navigate through. She stopped and considered her options. She could try and pass or she could leave her car and walk the rest of the way. Wading through didn't hold much sway, but neither did the idea of leaving her car. She took a deep breath, steered to the side, the shallowest part, and then drove straight ahead.

Midway through the puddle, the car seemed to slow down. She pressed the accelerator, it choked and then sputtered. Eventually she made it through the rest of the way. It was getting scary and she was getting more and more nervous. "That's it. Time for a distraction," she muttered.

To ease her nerves, she reached over and turned on the radio, finding the Holy Terror still on. He was issuing his top ten How to Get Through a Hurricane tips.

According to him, she had food, wine and a cozy place to relax, so all she needed was a man. "No, strike that," she said aloud. "All I need is Stephen."

Holy Terror repeated the warnings, then he opened the line to callers. Several people called in with additional helpful hints, while others gave on-the-scene flash flooding reports for local residents.

Mia consider calling in a few flooded roads then remembered she'd never charged her cell phone battery. Then it hit her. She could charge it from her car battery. She reached over and pulled the adapter from the small compartment, dug out her cell phone then connected the two.

Seconds later the car rocked. Mia gripped the steering wheel as the car splashed through another puddle. Water sprayed up against the driver's side window causing her to jump. "Okay, time to get home a little quicker," she said, just as Holy Terror promised something slow and easy to take everyone's mind off the weather.

"This is for all the lovers out there weathering the storm in each other's arms. Tonight is the night not to tell, but to show that special someone how you feel about them. So, brothers, while Hurricane Ana is out there banging on the door, you take care of your

business and take your special lady in your arms. Give her love. Show her how much you care. And, ladies, you know what to do. Me, well, let's just say I'm doing just fine right here. Come here, baby. Let's get it on."

His voice was gentle and promising, making her wonder if Holy Terror had a special someone right there in the booth with him. The song began playing. It was an old one, Marvin Gaye singing his classic "Let's Get It On." Her smile broadened as she immediately began feeling the music and listening to the words as if they were detailed instructions. Then she sang along, nodding her head and moving to the easy flow of the soulful rhythm.

"Yes," she said softly in agreement. Marvin was right. His words were exactly what she was feeling. She *had* been holding back too long searching for someone and now here he was there for her. She nodded agreeing completely. What was wrong about her being with him, loving him? Nothing. She wanted him and he wanted her, so what was she waiting for?

As the song faded she heard it come back on again. She listened again singing louder this time. It was played two more times and each time she affirmed more and more that she wanted to do exactly what Marvin suggested. By the time the song ended, Mia realized she was driving calmly. Marvin and Holy Terror had gotten her all the way home. The song had taken her mind off the weather; unfortunately it put her mind squarely on something—or rather someone—else. Stephen.

Mia pulled into the driveway, grabbed her supplies and groceries and ran into the house. She put everything away, jumped into a cool shower then dressed in her brand-new loungewear. No expectations, she promised herself. If he came, he came. But she knew she was lying. She wanted him there with her. She grabbed her charged cell and called her sister at work. Nya picked up immediately. "Hey, how's it going down there?" she asked.

"Not too bad. I went into town this morning and picked up some supplies."

"How long are you going to be down there?"

"I have no idea. Long enough to settle this, I hope. The clerk's office was closed again today, so it looks like I'm here for a few more days as least."

"You must be bored stiff." When Mia started laughing, Nya asked, "Wait a minute. Is the cop still around?"

"He did spend the night here."

"For real?" She started laughing. "Did you enjoy yourself?"

"As a matter of fact, I did, several times. Actually, I lost count." They laughed.

"You go, girl. Way to take care of yourself." Nya continued to laugh heartily. "Okay, okay, details. What's his full name? I need to look him up on the scanner." The scanner was what Nya called the magazine personal database. It listed just about everybody imaginable, noteworthy or notorious, and anyplace in between.

Mia sighed. "His full name? Believe it or not, I have no idea."

"Are you serious? Well, it was a one-night stand so as long as he doesn't get all clingy, then I guess it's okay. You had your fling and got your engine fired up a few times. So you don't see him again. It was fun while it lasted, right?"

"Actually, I just might see him again."

"Okay, that's different. What do you know about him?"

"He was born in Miami, his grandfather is the sheriff of Key West. He's a deputy sheriff following in the family business as it were. His name is Stephen and that's it. Oh, and he got hurt in an accident last week."

"Not a lot to go on, but let's see," Nya said. Mia heard her quick typing then a brief pause. "Okay, I have a Deputy Sheriff Esteban Morales, does that sound right?" she asked.

"Esteban is Stephen in Spanish," Mia said.

"Oh, that's right. I forgot you speak fluent Spanish. So that's him then. Okay, let's see, Monroe County Sheriff's office protects and serves all of the Florida Keys, from Florida City to Key West…over two million visitors each year…there's the regular citation awarded stuff and some photos. Oh, is this him?"

"Nya, how am I supposed to know? I have my laptop, but no electricity, remember? Describe him."

"This guy has a bronze caramel complexion, he's clean-shaven, has very short hair. Ooh, nice, he's built like an African warrior, drop-dead gorgeous and looking just too fine in this white shirt and black pants uniform. Also he's got dark, soulful eyes that make you want to dive in and never come up for air."

"Sounds about right," Mia said.

"Girl, he is gorgeous," Nya said. "I'm sending this profile to Janelle. Okay, here's something interesting— photos for the special weapons and tactic division."

"He's SWAT?" Mia asked, surprised.

"No," Nya said, "but there are a few seriously attractive men that are. I think I'd better plan myself a trip to the Keys." Nya chuckled and Mia just shook her head. Her sister was too outrageous.

They continued talking about Stephen awhile longer,

then the weather, Paradise Island and finally Stephen again. Later, after hanging up, Mia skimmed through the local newspaper. The hurricane, of course, was front-page news. Then turning the pages she was surprised to see a picture of Stephen. The article was about his heroic rescue a week ago and the citation he would receive. The caption read, "Local hero Deputy Sheriff Esteban Morales to be honored at Terrence Jeffries's Club Hurricane tomorrow night."

With a glass of wine in hand, from a bottle she picked up earlier, Mia went into the living room, grabbed her book and started reading. The battery-operated lamp she bought worked perfectly. It was just bright enough for her to read in comfort. But as soon as she turned a few pages, she started getting sleepy. Having not slept much the night before, she felt her eyes grow heavy and soon she fell asleep. Her dreams came in a kaleidoscope of images all centered on Deputy Sheriff Esteban Morales.

All warnings had been heeded. Roads were blocked and shelters were full. Now Stephen could finally get to Mia. He drove directly to Leo's house. The first thing he noticed was that one side of the front yard was beginning to flood. It wasn't an unusual occurrence when it rained too much and too hard. He often helped Leo pump water out of the yard. But not now. It was raining too hard and the wind had gotten stronger. Ana was definitely not finished.

He ran along the saturated paved walkway, then cut across to the flooded inset stepping stones. He hurried up the steps to the front door and knocked. There was no answer. He'd seen Mia's car parked out front so he knew she was home. He knocked again and then checked the doorknob. It turned easily. He shook his head making a mental note to remind her to secure the locks, something he always warned Leo to do, as well.

Inside he looked around. The room was dark, but he saw Mia instantly. She looked cozy and content curled up in her father's huge chair. He removed his wet raincoat and walked over to her. As he looked down at her, his heart lurched and a muscle in his neck tensed. She was the only woman to elicit such a powerful reaction from him. She was his Mia, the woman he had adored for so long.

She had told him not to come, but how could he not?

At that moment she was his and he drank in everything about her. She had on a sleeveless cream-colored dress that came down to her red toenails. It buttoned up the front and was opened just enough that he could see the sweet swell of her breasts and the luscious curve of her thighs. His already hard erection jumped of its own volition at just seeing her brown skin.

He inhaled quickly and licked his lips, but his mouth was too dry to suffice. She took his breath away. "Slowly," he whispered, cautioning himself, mindful of his promise. He knelt down to her, taking in the visual perfection of the woman of his fantasies as she slept.

Mia opened her eyes slowly, feeling her dream turn to reality. Stephen stood before her. Wordlessly he knelt down to her, his eyes never leaving hers. She read his intention there. Then in an instant his mouth was on her everywhere, kissing, licking, tasting, arousing her body's senses to passionate madness. She gasped and moaned enjoying the dreamlike sensations of his lustful hunger. Then he leaned back and smiled.

He reached out and began unbuttoning her dress

slowly, seductively revealing her nakedness to his pleasure. She waited impatiently, longing for the seconds to pass quickly, yet wanting this moment to last forever. When the fabric finally parted, her body heated to molten lava as she watched his dark eyes burn over her skin. He touched her nipple, and she trembled. Watching intently she saw his finger run down the front of her stomach then drift between her legs. She gasped as his fingers brushed her wetness. Her legs parted instinctively for him.

He leaned closer, his mouth hovering just inches from hers. The kiss captured her, freezing and burning her at the same time. His tongue delved deep, taking her breath away. She inched closer, wanting all of him. His hands caressed her, feeling her heavy breasts, her quivering stomach, and the oh-so-sweet wetness he loved to fondle. She called out his name as his lips followed the path his hand had just taken. He kissed down, down, deeper to her core, her treasure.

She lay there enjoying his masterful quest. Her body shook in anticipation. She watched anxiously as he parted her legs and leaned down to playfully lick and kiss her inner thigh. Every nerve ending jumped and every brain cell scrambled while she waited for that instant when he'd put his mouth on her feminine core. He raised her hips, kissing her there just seconds before his tongue entered her. She screamed in ecstasy as his hands held her hips in place and his mouth and tongue savored the sweet treasure she opened up to him.

Stroking her throbbing nub with his tongue, he ravaged and worshipped her body with unrestrained fervor. Her legs quivered uncontrollably. No one could possibly endure such intense pleasure at one time. She heard her own shrieks of pleasure building inside as her climax inched closer to the pinnacle. His gentle licking and lustful sucking stoked her closer and closer to the edge. Then at last she reached a climax so fierce she feared her rigid body would shatter in pieces. But he didn't stop. His hands covered her breasts, tweaking her hardened nipples as she came again and again, trembling, shaking, shuddering, quivering and writhing in mind-blowing pleasure.

She held her breath as her heart pounded, ready to explode. She couldn't think or speak. All she could do was lie there and want him more. "Stephen," she muttered, "Stephen."

Mia opened her eyes. Stephen was there kneeling, but he hadn't even touched her. She was dreaming. He leaned over and instantly took her mouth in heated possession, filling her quickly. Breathlessly she obliged, readily filling his with her searching tongue. When the kiss ended she was breathlessly exhausted. "Stephen," she panted, with bated breath. "I thought you were…"

"That must have been some dream," he said, smiling easily.

Mia closed her eyes and shook her head slowly. "It was."

"Are you okay?" he asked, softly stroking her bare arms.

She sleepily half smiled. "I'm blissfully confused. I've never had a dream that vivid before. It was so real."

He returned her sly smile with one of his own. "Looks like I got here just in time. I specialize in the blissfully confused."

"Do you really?" she asked. He nodded then kissed her hand. She smiled happily. "Deputy Sheriff Esteban

Morales." When he tilted his head curiously, she told him, "my sister looked you up on the Internet, plus there was also a nice article about you in the newspaper yesterday."

"I forgot all about that."

"Esteban," she repeated. "I like it. So what should I call you, Stephen or Esteban?"

"Call me yours."

She smiled. "What am I going to do with you?"

"Love me," he said plainly.

She saw the truth and sincerity in his eyes as a fire burned deep in her own heart, one she had never felt burning before. It certainly hadn't burned for Neal. She understood instantly. Stephen wasn't joking. He wanted her to love him. She reached out and touched his face gently. "I don't even know you."

"Yes, you do, better than you think."

Mia nodded. On some level he was right. It was as if she'd known him all her life. In just hours she felt a connection so deep, so strong and intense that it seemed to overpower time itself. Her mind told her one thing, but her heart compelled her to another. This man had been created for her. He was meant to love her, protect her and honor her. She was filled with sudden warmth that quickly turned to heated desire. "Make love to me, Esteban."

"We need to talk first. There are things you need to know."

"Okay, so tell me later," she said, as she began unbuttoning his shirt. When she finished she pulled the hem out of his pants then began undoing his belt. The heaviness of his gun weighed it down instantly. She moved it aside and began unfastening and unzipping his pants. Her nimble fingers brushed against his arousal.

He jerked back, grabbing her hands and holding her still. "Mia, I need to tell you this."

"After."

"No, now," he insisted.

"Now?" she questioned, sure he would change his mind. "Are you sure?" He nodded decisively, releasing her. She reached up and began unbuttoning her dress. "I read chapter fourteen," she purred. When the last button was undone, she stood before him and opened her long dress, completely naked. She saw him close his eyes, clearly weakening. "Are you sure?" she asked him again.

Stephen grabbed her hips and brought her body to his face. His hands gripped her buttocks, squeezing and rubbing her. He inhaled deep, filling his lungs with the scent of her essence. His body was too hard and his love for her too wanting. They both knew that making love was a foregone conclusion, but he wanted to take it slow and savor every second, every inch of her. He had no idea how he'd manage when he wanted her so bad.

He kissed her stomach possessively, passionately, sealing the fate they both knew wouldn't be ignored. She belonged to him and he belonged to her. As fiery passion consumed them, his passion deepened, taking her to the place she longed to be. He reached up to caress her breasts. She covered his hands and massaged her breasts along with him. "Mia."

"Esteban, I want you to feel me and taste me," she said, smiling brazenly down at him. He grabbed her hips and sat her down, then opened her legs wide. He smiled like a man given a glimpse of heaven. His mouth came down to cover her. She closed her eyes, held his neck and leaned her head back, biting her nails into his shoulders, waiting for his love to come to her. It did. In blinding climax, over and over again. In lustful passion that took her to that wonderful place he promised.

Afterward, they lay together on the sofa, his shirt still open as well as her dress. He held her tight, stroking her arm and back, occasionally kissing the top of her head. "How do I get you out of my system?" he asked, almost rhetorically.

"You don't," she said, smiling to herself.

Chapter 12

Stephen woke up and reached out for Mia. She wasn't there. He instantly sat straight up and looked around the living room. It was dark. They'd fallen asleep on the sofa, but now she was gone. "Mia," Stephen called out.

"Up here," she yelled down.

He grabbed a flashlight and hurried up to the attic finding her lifting a plank of wood. "What are you doing?" he asked, hurrying over to help her. She knelt down to a wooden box, opened the lid and looked inside. Although the room was illuminated by a portable lamp, he held the flashlight directly above her.

"I just remembered my dad jury-rigging this system years ago. I forgot all about it. It's supposed to be self-sustaining especially in high winds. The stronger the outside wind, the more the air circulates inside. It's like a jacked-up windmill. Hot air escapes as hurricane winds increase. The thing is, you can't open it too wide or for too long or the strong winds will tear the roof off." She pushed the last panel to the side and instantly a cool breeze hit them. "Hey, it works," she rejoiced, proud of her accomplishment. "Perfect." The makeshift system made an instant impact.

"Wow, that's amazing," Stephen said, standing. "I had no idea Leo was an inventor."

She recovered the system then looked up. Stephen held his hand out to help her stand. She grasped it and was quickly whisked into his arms. They stood close until he released her. "My dad called himself a modern-day Renaissance man."

Stephen smiled. "Yeah, I remember that phrase well."

A moment of reflection passed over them. Mia smiled thinking of all the things her father had done. Then feeling remorseful, she turned and walked away. "So Natalia's your cousin, huh?" Mia began.

Stephen nodded. "Our mothers are sisters."

"She seems nice. She knows a lot about the local goings on. What does she do here?"

"She's a deputy sheriff like me, and our own resident social worker and psychologist."

"Impressive, and her husband doesn't mind what she does for a living?"

"She's not married."

"Oh, sorry, I just assumed…"

"Because she's pregnant?" he asked. Mia nodded. "Family is very important to Natalia; to all of us. She decided that the special man she wanted in her life didn't exist, so she chose to start a family alone. She visited a sperm bank on the West Coast and came back pregnant, twice."

"Twice? You mean she's having twins?"

"No, she already has a son, Brice, who's two years old. She's expecting a second child with the same sperm donor. She wanted her children to be truly blood-related."

"So the donor doesn't know who she is or that he has two sons?"

"No, she bought the sperm outright. She didn't want any legal problems with the donor later."

"You mean problems like him wanting his sons?" she asked. He nodded. "Why would he, I mean if he donated his sperm, then that's it, right?"

"Not necessarily. There are always loopholes. By purchasing the sperm she's able to sure up as many as possible."

"When you say it like that it sounds so clinical. But still she's an amazing woman with a lot of courage."

"Actually she's a pain, but that's a whole other story."

Mia laughed as her stomach growled. "Oops, I think I'm starved. Are you hungry?" she asked.

"Not necessarily for food," he said, reaching out, grabbing her and pulling her close. She batted his hand away playfully.

"I'm gonna find us something to eat. I went to the grocery store earlier and got some canned food."

"I have a better idea. How about a lobster feast?"

"Don't play with me. I just told you I'm starved."

"Come on, dinner should be just about ready." He took her hand and she followed him downstairs then outside. The weather was still horrible with heavy rains, thunder rumbles and high gusting winds.

"There's no way I'm going out to dinner in that mess."

"We won't have to," he said. The cooler he expected

to be beside the door was there safe and secure. He grabbed the handles and brought it inside to the kitchen. Mia followed, squealing like a kid at Christmas ready to open her first present.

He opened the lid. Inside were two sides of the insulated cooler, one hot and one cold. Stephen opened the hot side and pulled out two large cooked Maine lobsters, steaming hot corn on the cob and baby new potatoes. From the cold side he pulled out jumbo shrimp cocktail and two slices of key lime pie.

Mia laughed with delight. "I can't believe it. Where did you get this?"

"A friend of mine owns a nightclub. He has connections, and then another friend dropped it off at the door."

"They must be really good friends," Mia said.

"The best. We're like brothers. We all went to the University of Miami together," he said.

She popped the cork on the bottle of wine she'd opened earlier and then grabbed two plastic cups, plates and a bunch of napkins. "Where shall we eat?" she asked.

The choice was simple. The house was like an oven everywhere except in the attic where the wooden slats filtered in a refreshing hurricane breeze. Mia spread a blanket and sheet on her father's old desk. They pulled up a couple of chairs and enjoyed their feast. Afterward, they sat talking and sipping wine.

"You have to thank your friend," Mia said. "This meal was delicious."

"I'll pass it on. I'm sure Lucas and the Holy Terror would appreciate the compliment."

"The Holy Terror, as in the DJ on WLCK? He's your friend?" She thought for a moment. "Oh, right! I heard him give you a shout-out on the radio."

Stephen nodded. "Yeah, Terrence Jeffries and Lucas McCoy are my best friends from college."

"Wow, Terrence's career on the gridiron is legendary. How many times was he in the Super Bowl?"

Stephen chuckled. "Wait, you're a football fan?"

"Are you kidding? I'm a huge football fan, thanks to my dad. During the season Dad and I would call each other and talk the entire game. Before unlimited calling, the long-distance phone bills were insane. When I was a teenager, I remember my grandmother threatening to send me to stay with him during the season just so we'd stop killing her phone bill." She laughed, and Stephen joined in.

"You two must have been scary."

"We were, believe me. It's funny that we only called each other during football games."

"You didn't communicate anytime except then?" he asked.

"We did. We just didn't call. We wrote letters. Every week or so a letter would come. I have hundreds and hundreds of letters. It was our thing—we wrote to each other. When I was young I couldn't wait until the mailman arrived. I knew there'd be a letter for me from my dad."

"That's pretty cool. It explains a lot."

"So, what about your friend Lucas McCoy? How does he fit in all this?" she said.

"Lucas delivered the cooler."

"In this weather, please thank him for me."

"I will, if I can catch up with him," Stephen said, shaking his head woefully. "The man has a huge heart. I hate to see him go down like this. People take advantage of him, specifically his fiancée from New York. At least once a month she promises to visit, but she never comes. I don't know how he puts up with it."

"Maybe he just loves her," Mia said.

"Maybe once, but I don't think so anymore. We'll see."

"I can relate to your friend. Thinking you're in love can make you do all kinds of stupid stuff, believe the wrong things, trust the wrong people. You give your heart and watch someone else break it with lies. I gave up on love."

"Don't give up on love, Mia. It'll never give up on you. You have to believe that or none of this will ever matter. Love doesn't pretend or fool you. Love is trust, understanding and forgiveness. Most importantly, love is unconditional. Sometimes things happen for reasons we don't see or understand. Afterward we learn lessons, and then we're able to move on. Don't give up." He seemed to almost plead his case.

She nodded, feeling his words sink deep into her heart. "So," she offered, sensing a change in the conversation was needed, "tell me about little Esteban growing up in Miami."

"I have a better idea. You tell me about Mia growing up here."

Mia smiled happily. "Summers here with my dad were the best times of my life. They were magical. I usually came down for about six or eight weeks. He'd have every day planned out. We'd go fishing, or snorkeling, or go to baseball games, or play tennis. Sometimes we'd just go to the movies or walk on the beach collecting seashells."

She laughed out loud. "Oh man, I remember this one time we were walking on the beach early in the morning and I saw this beautiful rock on the sand. It was amber, smooth and frosted. Dad told me it was a mermaid's tear. I was young, so I believed him. For years I collected mermaid's tears. I found them in all colors, blue, green, amber and even clear. Once I even found a red one, although I still think my dad planted if for me to find. Red ones are extremely rare. Anyway, it wasn't until I was a teenager that I found out that they were just regular broken glass pieces tumbled and smoothed by the ocean and sand."

"Sea glass," he said.

She nodded. "Yeah, that's right. Dad kept my jar of sea glass for years. Every summer I'd come back and start collecting all over again. There must have been a hundred pieces in that jar. One year Dad and I actually made a mermaid's tears necklace. I wore it that whole summer." She sighed dreamingly. "I loved that necklace, maybe more because we made it together. Anyway, the necklace broke one winter and I never made another one. The last time I was here, a few years ago, my jar was still sitting in the living room. It's gone now. I guess he got rid of it."

"Leo saved everything. I'm sure it's safe."

She shook her head sadly. "I looked. It's not here." She looked around and sighed. "I'm really gonna miss this place."

"What do you mean?"

"I came down to save it, though now it's probably too late. The bank's already foreclosing on it."

"It's not too late."

She nodded slowly. "I was told when they called that someone's already put a bid on it. I don't have the kind of money to give the bank to pay it off and I'm not asking my family for it."

"The house will be safe, just like your mermaid's tears."

"No, and maybe that's how this story is supposed to end. See, Dad and I argued a couple of years ago. We didn't agree on something and our relationship just drifted apart. No, that's not true. I let it drift apart. He called, but I wouldn't pick up. I was so angry at him. I was stubborn, just like him," she said softly. "I was stupid and he just stopped calling. I know I should have been here, but I—" She stopped as her voice was getting choked up.

"Mia, I told you, Leo understood. He loved you so much."

"No, you don't understand. He called me," she whispered, thickly. "It was…I guess a few days before he died. I didn't take his call. Now I just keep seeing him here alone. It hurts so much inside." She bowed her head tearfully.

Stephen wrapped his arms around her, comforting her. "He wasn't alone. I was here when he died. His last words were for you. He loved you fiercely and wanted you to know that he was wrong."

"No, that's just it. He was right all along. I should have listened to him. Now it's too late. I'm so sorry. I'm just so sorry."

Stephen held her tight and rocked her gently, feeling her pain and reliving his own. "You are so blessed to have had Leo as your father. He was the kind of dad I dreamed of having growing up, someone to hang with and just know that I was alive. My mother was there, and my sisters, but it wasn't the same. She was great, fantastic, but she wasn't my father.

"Meeting Leo made me realize what fatherhood is supposed to be. Just listening to the stories he told about you made me know what kind of father I want to be and what kind of man I am."

She sat up. "This isn't fair. You know so much about me, but I don't know anything about you."

"My life isn't very interesting, believe me."

"Okay, so I gather you weren't close to your dad growing up. What else? What about your mother?"

"Actually it's the other way around. It was more like he wasn't close to me. My grandfather is from Cuba. He grew up poor and worked hard to succeed. Once he made it, he never stopped working. My father did the same, but growing up with money made him more determined to keep what he had. Success became everything and anything, and anyone that threatened that success he crushed by any means necessary. I found myself becoming just like them, like him, following in their footsteps."

"I find that hard to believe."

"It's true. I was in the family business until a few years ago. I couldn't do it anymore, even at the risk of walking out on him and my family."

"So you're not close with your family now?"

"I'm close to my sisters and mother and her side of the family. I'm even close to my dad's side of the family, but…"

"But not your dad?" she asked. He shook his head. "Stephen, don't be like me. Don't let one argument keep you apart. When it's too late, it's too late. Talk to him, make peace. Whatever you argued about is long over, I'm sure. Think about it, okay?"

He nodded, suddenly finding himself lost in thoughts he hadn't considered in years. Maybe Mia was right. Maybe it was time to put everything aside and open his heart to his father again.

"After my father died, my fiancé took care of everything. He told me he hired a property management company to care for the house. Apparently he didn't. I called them and they said that they never even heard of me, him or the house." She didn't have to tell him, but she wanted to.

"Where's your fiancé now?"

"Married to somebody else, a coed at the college we teach at." She sighed heavily. "He betrayed me just like my dad said he would. He told me not to trust Neal. That's what the argument was about. I defended Neal." She shook her head woefully. "But my father was right all along."

"So the house had foreclosed and gone to auction."

"There's an outstanding property tax and double mortgage. The house was paid for, but my dad took out two mortgages for some reason. It's so strange. I have no idea why he would need so much money before he died." She smiled. "Anyway, it's funny, but being here with you, knowing you and knowing that you and my dad were close, makes me feel really close to him. It's like having a part of my dad here with me, in you."

"Do you still love your fiancé?" Stephen asked.

"No, in fact I don't think it was ever love. I think it was more like being comfortable and taking the next practical step. His mother is friends with my mother, so it seemed logical. I had a hard time at first. I doubted everything about myself."

Stephen smiled and nodded. "Leo once told me that you were bold and brave and could handle just about anything that came your way, even your ex."

"I guess I forgot how to be me."

"No, you didn't. Everything that's happened between us has proved that you are still that woman." He smiled. "I saw you," he said cryptically. She looked at him questioningly and he explained, "At Leo's memorial service, I saw you there. You were with two women."

She nodded. "My sisters, Nya and Janelle."

"And someone else," he prompted.

"Neal, Neal Bowes, my now ex-fiancé," she said.

"I assumed as much."

"Why didn't you say something, or come up and introduce yourself? I would have liked to have met you. Dad didn't have many friends, you know that. It would have been nice to meet one."

"It wasn't the right time," he said.

"You're a really good man, Stephen. So why aren't you married?"

"I've been looking for the right woman."

"And what's the right woman like?"

"She's like you, Mia."

Mia's heart skipped a beat and her stomach fluttered a thousand times over. She tried to smile, but she wasn't sure if she did. All she knew was she felt something inside let go, as if it had been held tight for years. She hoped he wasn't just being kind. But thankfully she was saved by the bell, or rather Stephen's cell phone, which was also a walkie-talkie. He answered.

It was dispatch asking him to stop by one of the shelters in the area. Apparently there was trouble and he was the closest officer since flooding blocked most of the other patrol officers closer to town. He agreed, then disconnected. "I don't know how long this is going to take."

"That's okay. I'll see you tomorrow," she said. He

stood and began to clear the dishes. "No, don't bother with this. I'll take care of it."

"Believe me, you don't want this trash around here in this heat," he said. Together they gathered the trash and loaded it back into the cooler.

Downstairs he gathered his belongings as Mia waited by the front door.

"Esteban, tonight was wonderful. I had a good time. Thank you so much." She tipped up on her toes and kissed him sweetly.

He shook his head slowly and grabbed her possessively, pulling her against his body.

"Baby, that's no way to say goodbye to a cop." He kissed her long and hard, devouring her whole and sending shock waves through every part of her body.

He left and twenty minutes later Mia was still feeling the effects of his kiss. Now upstairs in the attic, she folded the sheet and blanket then sat at her father's desk and looked around. She was thinking about her conversation with Stephen. She felt so close to him, perhaps because he was close to her father. Whatever the reason her feelings were getting stronger. She'd fallen in love with him.

Chapter 13

Stephen helped at the shelter and then headed to the local hospital. When he finally left, in the early hours of the morning, he drove past Leo's house. He looked up at the darkened facade but then continued to his home. Going to Mia would only mean making love to her all night, and although that would be a blissfully pleasurable experience, he needed space tonight. He needed to control and focus his thoughts. He was no closer to resolving his feelings than before she arrived. She had to be told the truth and his time was running out.

He'd known that the foreclosure and impending auction would prompt Mia to come down here. He'd figured it was his opportunity to once and for all get her out of his system. He'd even thought that if he had her physically, that would crush the intense longing he'd felt for her for so long. But he was wrong. Their physical intimacy only made him want her more. His feelings weren't based on the physical with Mia. Apparently they never were.

Given the morning off, he woke up late, showered, and then went out onto his deck overlooking the angry Gulf. The storm had crossed Florida, and then headed out to sea, and now it just seemed to hover in scattered array. He knew exactly how that felt. How do you tell the woman you love that you intentionally ruined her father, diminished his life's work, discredited and publicly humiliated him? How do you tell her that afterward, you tricked her into coming down here? And how do you then expect her to love you back?

"You don't," he said, answering his own rhetorical question.

Not wanting to think anymore, he went back into the house to get dressed.

His home was classic Key West conch style, large and accessible, built on a ridge overlooking Mallory Square. It was within easy walking distance of Leo's home, but it was far grander in style, size and character. Built just a year and a half ago, it was completely modern with every conceivable convenience, including an outdoor kitchen and terrace overlooking the Gulf of Mexico, which afforded him spectacular sunsets. He went down to the garage and turned on the generator, which he'd timed to power down overnight.

In the kitchen he grabbed a large glass of orange juice then sat out on the balcony watching the angry waves crash and churn the sea. When his cell phone rang, he expected it to be dispatch, but it was Terrence. "Hey, what's up?" he asked his friend.

"How was your seafood feast last night?" Terrence asked.

"Perfect. Thanks again for your help with that."

"I presume your lady was duly impressed, and that you told her everything." When Stephen didn't reply, Terrence said, "You didn't tell her, did you?"

"No, I couldn't. We wound up talking about fathers and our growing-up years. She still feels guilty about Leo."

"And *you* still feel guilty about Leo. That should make you the perfect pair. Man, listen to me, tell the woman. This isn't something you want her to find out on her own. Leo understood and forgave you. Why can't you forgive yourself? Tell her."

"I will," Stephen said. "So what about you and Sherrie?"

"Let's just say we're seeing more than eye to eye."

Stephen chuckled. "Excellent news. Anything happening with Lucas lately?"

"Nah, man, his fiancée is supposed to be coming, but with the hurricane, who knows? I guess we'll see what happens."

"I hope it works out for him," Stephen said sincerely.

"Ditto, a'ight, gotta jet, I have to get back on the air. Anything new happening out there you want me to pass on to the listeners?"

"Remind them to keep their pets inside. We're picking up quite a few with tags. Plus I hear Domino is still out there doing his thing." The dog always got out during storms, and afterward there was a mini population explosion.

"Got it. You take care," Terrence said.

"You, too, man. Later."

Stephen hung up and considered his friend's advice. He knew Terrence was right. He needed to talk to Mia. He grabbed his bag, tossed it in the back of his car then drove over to Leo's place. There was no time like the present.

Mia slept upstairs in the attic, the coolest place in the house. When she awoke shortly after dawn, she realized that last night was the first night she hadn't spent with Stephen since she'd met him. Of course she wondered and worried about him until late, eventually falling asleep reading some of her father's journals.

After getting washed and dressed, she went into town and did a quick drive by of the county clerk's office. As she expected, since it was Saturday, it was closed. She continued to the grocery store, but the shelves were basically empty. As a last resort she walked to the coffee shop. It was open and the aroma of freshly brewed coffee made her stomach growl. She sat with a blueberry muffin and coffee and read the local newspaper.

"Mia, right?"

Mia looked up, first seeing a rounded tummy, then a smiling face. "Yes, hi, Natalia, right?"

"You remembered."

Mia saw that she had a small white bakery bag and a cup of something in her hands. "Would you like to join me?"

"Thanks." Natalia sat and sipped her hot tea. "I'm so glad my sister decided to get one of those giant generators for the coffee shop a few years back. I don't know what I'd do without my tea and Danish."

"Your sister owns this bakery?" Mia asked.

Natalia nodded as she opened her white bag, then pulled out a cherry Danish and dug in. After one big luscious bite she smiled. "Man, I've been craving these things all morning."

"When are you due?" Mia asked.

"In two months, but it feels like I'm due next week. I know every pregnancy is different, but I swear it feels like I have a whole hockey team in here." They chuckled.

"So, you're Stephen's cousin," Mia said, opening a dialogue.

Natalia nodded. "Yeah, our moms are sisters. Didn't he tell you?"

"Yes, I guess I just feel better having it come from you."

"Been there, done that," Natalia said. "The cheating, lying, backstabbing, jerk of a boyfriend," she expounded. "I assume that's why you asked."

"That's exactly why I asked. I guess I have trust issues."

"Tell me about it. That's why I've decided to go solo."

"Solo?"

"Sperm bank."

"That sounds so…" Mia began, but stopped, not knowing how to end the comment without sounding judgmental or condescending.

"Different? It is. But I was tired of waiting for some Prince Charming that may or may not come into my life." She gently patted her protruding stomach and smiled. "This way I have all I need. I have a son, Brice, and I'll soon have another son. I'll just be both mother and father."

"I'm sure Stephen will be there to help, plus, didn't you mention before that you had brothers?" Mia said. "So, you won't be alone. You'll have plenty of help." She paused a moment. "To tell you the truth, I envy you."

"Me, why?" Natalia asked.

"You knew what you wanted and you got it."

"You don't know what you want or rather *who* you want, Mia?"

Mia smiled and shook her head. She'd forgotten how intuitive Natalia was. "Stephen," Mia said. "We've been hanging out lately, and I'm getting confused. It's only been two days and already I'm feeling too close."

"What's too close? Is that a bad thing? Most women I know would love to feel 'too close.'"

"Can I ask you something, between us?" Mia asked. Natalia nodded. "Is he for real?"

Natalia chuckled. "Mia, believe me, Stephen is very much for real. Just hear him out and trust your heart. Everything isn't as bad as it seems. Know that sometimes it's even better in the end."

The two women sat silently for a few moments until Natalia dotted her lips with a paper napkin then stood. "I need to get back to the office. Take care, Mia. Trust your heart and you'll be just fine."

Mia smiled. "Okay, and thanks for the conversation."

"Just stop by anytime. I'm usually here or at dispatch."

After Natalia left, Mia sat awhile longer sipping her coffee until she recognized the woman who'd just come in. The day before Natalia had identified her as the court clerk. The woman went up to the counter, ordered her baked goods then headed to the door. Mia stepped up quickly. "Excuse me, Helen Parker?"

"Yes," the woman said turning to look at Mia questioningly.

"We met briefly yesterday with Natalia."

"I thought you looked familiar. Hi."

"Hi, Helen, my name is Mia James. My father was Leo James."

"Oh, right, we spoke on the phone. Good Lord, you came all the way down here after our conversation, didn't you?" she asked. "I'm so sorry, dear, I didn't mean for you to make a mad dash down here in the middle of a hurricane. Had I known you were going to do that I wouldn't have called you."

"That's quite all right. Helen, I wanted to talk to you about my dad's house. When will your office reopen?"

Helen looked at her watch. Mia looked at her intently hoping she'd open it like Natalia had said she might. "I'll tell you what, I have a few minutes, so why don't we hop over and see what's going on."

"That would be wonderful. Thank you so much, Helen. You have no idea how much I appreciate this."

Mia followed Helen to the office then to her desk. It was dark and there was no electricity. "No generator?"

"Not in the budget," Helen said. "I can't get on the computer, but just looking at the files it looks like you're going to do pretty well after the mortgage balances, taxes and liens are paid. You already have a buyer for the property."

"Liens?"

Helen looked back at the files and nodded. "Two."

Mia frowned. This was getting more and more detailed. But she'd have to think about that later. "Okay, now that's just it. I don't want to sell it. How do I stop the foreclosure?"

"Mia, I'm sorry you came all the way down here. At this point the property sale is imminent. There's no way to stop it unless you can settle the debt on the property, which is measurable. I'm afraid there's not much anyone can do. The bank has already called the loan and they have an interested buyer. I doubt they'll stop the process at this point. After all, they're in this to make money."

Mia felt as if she'd just been gut punched. At some point she was sure she stopped listening. She just nodded as Helen continued talking.

"Are you okay?" Helen asked.

"Do you know who the buyer is? Maybe I can talk to them."

"I'm sorry, the computers are all down, and ethically, there's no way I can give you that information."

Mia nodded. She took a deep breath and then let it out slowly. It wasn't Helen's fault. It wasn't the bank's fault. She should have listened to her father, but it was too late. The house was gone. "Thanks, Helen, I appreciate this."

After a while she got up and walked back to her car. She got in, started the engine and removed the attachment to her phone. It had charged and was now blinking. She had seven messages, four from Nya and two from Janelle and one from her mother. She decided to return their calls when she got back to the house. She really didn't feel like talking to anyone right now.

On the way out of town she saw the county sheriff's office. Without thinking, she pulled over and parked. She needed to talk to Stephen. She went inside and saw Natalia.

"Hi," Mia said, walking over to where Natalia stood. "Um, I was wondering, is Stephen around?"

"No, I'm afraid not. Is it an emergency?"

"No, just if you see him, tell him…" She paused and shook her head. "Never mind, forget it."

"Are you sure? I can call him if you'd like."

"No, that's not necessary. See you later."

She hurried out and quickly drove back to the house. She pulled into the driveway and just sat for a moment. The music lulled her awhile, but even with that she grew weary. Looking up at her father's house she knew that she was too restless to sit in a hot house and be reminded of what she'd lost. She got out, tossed her jacket on the seat then instead of going inside she walked down the street, around the corner, then down to the boardwalk and then to the pier.

She felt completely safe on the old but stable wooden planks, as did a number of like-minded adventurers who joined her there. They had all come out to witness the splendor of nature's rage. From the end of the pier the Gulf seemed massive. Waves churned and rolled, crashing against each other in a dramatic symphony of power and fury. Her heart soared at the spectacle. Compared to this, her life and everything else was insignificant.

Beneath the planks she heard the high tide roll in closer and closer. Just a few slabs of wood separated her from the raging water below. She stood at the rail, the wind gusting around her. An occasional spritz of seawater sprayed her face sending a refreshing tingle against her skin.

The rough and restless sea fought against itself. It seemed to be the same force fighting inside of her. She felt overjoyed and disheartened at the same time. She realized that she was in love with Stephen even as she'd lost her father's house. Like the sea, the power of love was strong, undeniable. How do you beat a force like that? she wondered.

* * *

Stephen knew it was her as soon as he saw the figure walking toward the pier. She wore a white dress with her back exposed. Long and flowing, the bottom half blew recklessly in the troubled breeze. She wore a white scarf around her neck and held sandals in her hand. Her hair was tossed erratically and her movements were slow and deliberate. She was beautiful. She had no idea he watched her, as he'd done many times before. Stephen opened the gate and like a moth to a flame, he headed right to her.

Bare chested and barefoot, he walked down the steps that led to the beach and boardwalk. His eyes were focused solely on Mia, his vision in white. When he got to the boardwalk she had already reached the end of the pier. She stood looking out at the water as the wind gusts swirled around her.

"You know you really shouldn't be out here like this. It's dangerous."

Mia smiled as the disconnected voice gently enveloped her even before he was close enough to touch her. She turned around and leaned back against the guardrail, her arms holding the metal bars firmly.

He looked down at her low-cut dress. Her breasts were moistened by the sprays of seawater. "You're wet," he said.

"Yes, I am. You know me so well," she said boldly, then smiled at seeing his expression when he realized his comment could be construed a number of different ways.

Stephen reached out, grabbed her waist and pulled her to his side. She leaned flush against his body and looked up into his dark midnight eyes as he wrapped his arms around her. She exhaled with extreme pleasure.

This was what she wanted at the end of the day. She wanted to be in Stephen's arms and let everything else that didn't matter just disappear. "You are so beautiful. Do you have any idea what you've done to me?" he whispered, before gently touching his lips to hers. "So what are you doing out here?" he asked her.

"I needed to escape for a while."

"Escape from what?"

"Life, I guess. I was just remembering when I used to come out here years ago," she began as she stepped out of his arms and walked over to the rail overlooking the beach and surf. He followed close and stood behind her, their bodies were pressed together as one. He wrapped his arms around her and she leaned back against him, the protective feeling warming her heart.

"When I was younger, Dad and I would walk the beach for hours. Then we'd sit. He'd write and I'd build a huge sand fortress around us so that we'd have to be there forever. I never wanted things to change or time to move on. But it didn't work. The unstoppable tide would always come in and destroy my world."

She turned to him and looked up into his eyes. "They're not black. I thought they were," she said.

"My eyes?" he asked. "No, I have very dark brown irises. They appear black at times, but they're really brown."

"One of probably a thousand things I don't know about you."

He leaned down and kissed her. When their lips parted he smiled lovingly. "Are you okay?" he asked. "You look sad."

"No, I'm not okay. It's one of those days," she said.

"Do you want to tell me about it?"

She shook her head, then turned and looked out to the darkening sky and angry waters. "The storm's picking up again," she said.

"You're right, it is." He nodded his head slowly, knowing that they were talking about two different storms. She wasn't ready to hear what he had to tell her. But he had no choice. It was time. "And it's going to be a bad one," he added.

"The surf is so mesmerizing. I could stand here for hours just watching its awesome power. It's scary and beautiful and tempting all at the same time."

He turned to follow her gaze. She was right. The fierce rage of water was hypnotic. They stood in silence looking out at the massive force, and Stephen could feel them lose themselves in their own thoughts as they let the power of the water and the storm on the horizon bring memories and banish fears.

"This is where it all began for me," he said, staring down the beach. She looked up at him. "See over there?" He pointed out over the diminishing dunes. "My great-grandfather came ashore right there."

"Came ashore from where?" she asked.

"Cuba. He came here years ago, long before communist tyranny. He was poor in Cuba, so when he saw the riches in America he was enamored. He never returned. He moved his family here and they became American citizens. My grandfather worked hard to have the American dream. He was a busboy, a waiter, a bellhop, he fished, he did any job he could. He saved and he eventually bought an old flophouse. When the land was developed, he sold it and made more money than he'd ever seen before. Then he bought an apartment building, and another one, and another one. It became a business.

"Later my father joined him and they purchased a hotel, then another one. In time the hotels got bigger and grander and the business became a hotel development company. My grandfather died, and eventually greed and deceit became the norm. I joined the family business right out of college."

"Wait, I thought the family business was law enforcement."

"That's my mother's family," he said. "Anyway, my father and I pushed further and further, getting more and more while never seeing that we were losing everything that really mattered. And now betrayal, lies and greed is the only legacy left. It's all there, just like a lousy made-for-TV movie." He took a deep breath and shook his head sadly. "The business took our honor and everything else. That's the Morales family history, my family."

"But you're not working with your father anymore, right? That's all behind you," she said. He nodded. "Tell me something. Who takes over the business in the future now that you're not there? Do you have brothers or sisters?"

"I have two younger sisters, but neither is interested in the hotel development business at this point."

"That means the family business will eventually die away," she said quietly.

"I didn't kill the business. My father did."

"But still…"

"The business is fine. Better than fine at this point."

"Are your parents still together?"

"My mother's name is Whitney Coles Morales. She was a fashion model years ago. She is still the most beautiful woman I know, present company excluded, of course." Mia smiled and blushed as he continued. "She loved my father fiercely. Through his flaws and arrogance, she only saw their love. Her influence on him was tremendous, but eventually it wasn't enough. They divorced.

"The strange thing is that my father still loves her. You can see it in his eyes and know that he's thinking about her. He even keeps her photo on his office desk."

"It sounds like that kind of love is pretty powerful," she said.

"It is. Come on, let's go. I need to show you something."

He took her hand and they began walking. When they got to the end of the pier he turned right instead of left. She stopped. "Wait, Dad's house is back that way," she said, looking toward the other direction.

"We're not going to your dad's house."

"So where are we going?"

"You'll see. Come on."

She stared at him oddly, but still followed. He had a troubling expression on his face. She knew instinctively that whatever he wanted to show her, she wouldn't like.

Chapter 14

They walked down the pier to the boardwalk then took a shortcut across the beach through to a narrow pass. They climbed steps leading to a private walkway, then a secluded entrance. They rounded several curves until they came to what looked like a large beach house. Stephen opened the back gate, took Mia's hand and led her up the back steps to his balcony. When they reached the upper level she turned and looked back.

It wasn't quite sunset, and even with the heavy cloud cover, the view took her breath away. It was astounding. "Wow, is this your house?" she asked. He nodded. "It's amazing." She was stunned by the sheer glamour and magnificence of his home.

"Come on, this way." He led her through the kitchen to the dining room then down through the sunken living room and finally to a large study. He turned on the light and walked over to the desk.

"Wait. How do you have electricity?"

"I have a generator."

"Stephen, this place is incredible."

"Thank you. A good friend of mine designed it."

"You're a cop. How can you afford all this?"

"I'm a cop with means. This was supposed to be my serenity at one time."

"Your serenity?"

He nodded. "I guess for a time it was. I'd work eighty-hour weeks then once every few months I'd retreat here to Key West. That's when I decided to build. I expected this to be the place where I'd find contentment."

"Was it?"

"No."

"Why not?" she asked.

"I started building it about five years ago. I stopped when I quit the business. I never intended to live here."

"Why not?"

"It's built with blood money."

"What do you mean, like drug money?" she asked, following him across the room to a large mahogany desk.

He didn't respond, he just opened the top center drawer and pulled out a folder filled with newspaper articles and handed it to her.

"What's this?" she asked.

"Read them."

"What are they?" She opened the folder and glanced at the byline. The top article was written by her father almost four years earlier. "My dad wrote these."

"Just read them." He pulled out the large comfortable swivel chair and gestured for her to sit behind the desk. She did. He turned the lamp on then walked out.

A short while later Mia walked out reversing the same path back to the kitchen. Stephen was standing on the balcony looking out. "You look peaceful," she said admiringly.

"Looks are deceiving," he said, turning and seeing the folder and article in her hand.

"I see my dad really did a hatchet job on your family business." Stephen nodded. "I suppose you had the IRS, INS and federal regulators on your back, not to mention the media." He nodded again. "My father was vigilant for a cause."

"He did what he thought was right," Stephen said.

"I'm sorry," she said softly, feeling the strain of being her father's daughter weigh heavily on her shoulders for the first time. Leo was a ferocious pit bull when he was on an investigative assignment. God help anyone he was going after. But for some reason this article seemed harsher than usual. This time, it was like a personal attack.

"Did you read them all?" he asked.

"No, I stopped after the first few. I got the general drift of his point. He alleged that your father bribed city officials and attempted to build hotels with low-grade material resulting in poor workmanship. Eventually there was a fire."

"The initial stage of construction was almost complete. We'd been approved up to that point. The first major assessment was to take place the following week. The fire happened that weekend. There was just a skeleton crew on site."

"Did anyone get hurt?" she asked.

"Three people were sent to the hospital with smoke

inhalation, two more with broken bones, having jumped from a platform. One man is still suffering through third-degree-burn surgeries."

"My dad claims in the articles that it was faulty subprime material that sparked the blaze."

"People could have died had that hotel continued to be built. I approved all the requisition orders. It was my fault."

"Did you know about the alleged bribes? Were you involved?"

"No, of course not," he said quickly.

"Then how could it have been your fault?" She paused and looked at him. "This is why you quit working with your father, isn't it?" she asked, holding the file out to him. He didn't respond. "My father mentioned you prominently in these articles. Stephen, I'm so sorry for what he did to you."

"Don't be. It was his job and he was right to do it."

"I don't know what to say."

"Don't say anything, Mia," he promised. "Just read everything in the file, all of it. You need to know everything."

"I don't need to read any more," she said.

"You need to read these. It's important. There's more to tell you, but I want to be here when you read them," he assured her.

"I will, later," she said softly as she reached behind her neck and unfastened the clasp, releasing the top of her dress. It slipped down to her waist and she helped it the rest of the way. She stepped out and stood there smiling, in sandals and white panties.

Stephen looked down the length of her body and forgot to breathe. She looked delicious and he was instantly hard.

"You once told me that it wasn't the right time to introduce yourself to me. I didn't agree with you then, but I do now. I'm glad you waited. Timing is everything, isn't it?"

"Mia," he began, his mouth as dry as Death Valley, "we can't do this now. You need to see the rest of the file."

"I will, later, but first…" She walked over to him and stood so close, the tips of her nipples brushed against his skin. Even that light touch was enough for them to pebble instantly. She saw him watch in rapt attention. "I take it you approve this time," she said, then wrapped her arms around his neck, pressing her body against his.

She kissed him hard, sealing herself to the intensity of feelings she had for him. There was no denying it any longer. She loved him and in that love she wanted to forget all this, her father, his father, the articles, everything. All she wanted was to love him and for him to love her back.

The kiss lasted an eternity. The fierceness of her driving hunger stoked her passion. He held on to her, gripping her bare back and grasping the nape of her neck to press her closer and deepen the kiss. The kiss was long and lustful, forging the passion that stirred in her. She touched his chest and smiled. She loved touching him, feeling him. Her nails skimmed across his skin, raking lightly. The back of her hand brushed his nipple. She noted that he stiffened.

Breathing hard, Stephen jerked back, setting her away from him. "Mia, I can't do this tonight," he rasped faintly.

She reached down and took hold of the steel hardness beaconing out to her and then smiled easily. "I think you can."

He took her hand away quickly before losing all control. "You don't understand." He looked into her eyes seeing love reflected back at him and the future he so desperately wanted with her. *Maybe she will understand. Maybe her love will forgive me.* His hunger was suddenly stoked beyond anything he'd ever experienced. He was hard as a rock and all he could think about was burying himself deep inside her body. He trembled as his penis throbbed and pulsated with need.

She stepped back and took his nipple into her mouth and sucked gently. His body tremored. She repeated the action and he shuddered. She nibbled him teasingly, then licked and suckled more. He grabbed her arms in an iron vise to hold her away. She looked up at him. His eyes were black as the storm raging in the distance. He had the strength, but she had his will.

"Let go, Esteban," she said sweetly, belying the insatiable intensity in her eyes. He released her instantly and she devoured his nipple again, this time with more fervor. She seemed to punish him for his impertinence. He shivered as his breathing increased. She felt his heart pound in his chest. The joy of controlling this man as he controlled her was exhilarating.

A deep throaty groan escaped him as he quickly lifted her up. Their mouths met in a staggering kiss. She wrapped her legs around his waist and he carried her, to where she had no idea. Seconds, moments or hours later, when their lips finally parted, she looked up, no longer seeing the overcast sky above her. She was in bed, lying down with Stephen hovering over her. She tossed her head back giving him full access to all of her. He readily accepted her invitation devouring as much of her as he could.

He greedily consumed one dark orb, suckling and drawing her deep into his mouth while caressing the other. She gasped, holding firm to his head and directing the pull of his mouth. The pleasure was mind-boggling, but she wanted even more. "Wait, wait," she panted.

He released her and leaned away, then rolled onto his back. She sat up and looked down at him. His eyes were closed and he was breathing hard. She looked around seeing that they were indeed in his bedroom lying on a large master bed. She saw his handcuffs on the dresser and decided to have a different kind of fun tonight. She got up.

"Where are you going?" he muttered.

"I'll be right back." Moments later she returned smiling menacingly as she got back on the bed. He opened his eyes seeing what she brought with her and knew exactly what she intended to do. She straddled him then lifted his hand above his head. She clicked one cuff onto his wrist. "I hope this is the key," she whispered in his ear just before she nibbled the lobe. He barely nodded. "Good." She threaded the chain part around the brass headboard. She drew his other hand up over his head and clicked the other cuff then placed the key on the table beside the bed. He lay helpless to her bidding and she liked it.

She sat back admiring her handiwork and wondering what to do first. He looked up at her, trusting her completely. She ran her finger over his lips, down his chin and over his shoulders then lower to his nipple. He gasped and squeezed his eyes tight as he called out her name repeatedly. She smiled broader. The power to make him call out to her was exquisite. She could get used to this.

She leaned over and licked the nipple. He bucked his hips almost tossing her off balance. She licked the other nipple, and he bucked again. She scratched her nails down his chest to his stomach then to the band of his sweatpants. She moved to the side and untied the string, then removed the sweats and boxer briefs, releasing his penis. He opened his eyes and she asked, "Condoms?"

He couldn't respond. He was teetering on dynamite ready to explode. The only thing holding him back was the sheer power of will and the need to see her explode along with him. She repeated her question, and he looked to the table beside the bed. As she reached across him to open the drawer, he leaned up and took her nipple into the warmth of his mouth. She gasped her surprise, but let him have his prize. Then breathlessly tormented she pushed back and leaned away. She opened the package and covered him, slowly with as much deliberate pleasure as she could give.

Stephen tensed as she straddled him again. "Mia," he said, and then managed to ramble a few inaudible words.

She didn't hear him, nor did she need to. Her thoughts were solely on the pleasure of his body. She ground her hips against his groin, pressing closer and feeling the hardness of his body respond with pulsating throbs.

He sizzled, groaning, feeling the need to let her dominate and do what she did so well. "Mia."

"Shh," she whispered in his ear. She kissed his chest and then came to his nipple again. "Do you like how this feels?" she asked, teasing him with her tongue. He didn't answer. She nibbled him again, and he tensed and rumbled deep. "I asked you a question, Esteban. *¿Hacen usted tienen gusto de cómo esto siente?*" He nodded weakly this time. *"Contésteme,"* she commanded. "Answer me."

"*Sí*," he replied.

"Good, do you want more?" she asked.

"Yes, *sí, más*."

She gave him more while delighting in her new role. She reached up and kissed his neck, his shoulders and down his chest, loving the taste of his mocha skin. Then, centering her passion on his nipples, she kissed then bit him, then licked his painful pleasure away. He groaned with each love bite. This was good, but now she wanted even more.

She sat up and placed her body on target. Without hesitation, she impaled her core onto him, sliding down onto his erection. She screamed at the exquisite pleasure of being filled. He was harder, longer, stronger than she'd ever felt before. He said something in Spanish, but she was long past listening to his words. It was his body that spoke to her now as her body spoke to him.

She surged in deeper covering him completely, feeling his penis penetrate deep into her body. She ground her hips, adding intensity to the sensation. Then she released and thrust again. Over and over, in and out, back and forth, she pounded into his rigid body, churning and grinding into him just as the menacing waves she'd seen earlier. The same awesome power was there building to an unimaginable climax.

She leaned down with her hands beside his chest, dipping her breasts teasingly as her hips rocked. Unable to touch her with his hands, he leaned up and took her into his mouth. Her hips pounded as his mouth suckled, the same rhythm, the same intensity, the same power. Each shuddered and writhed breathlessly building what would surely explode in blinding ecstasy.

The fierceness of their bodies connecting swelled

beyond all reason. She was coming hard; she could feel her stomach tighten and her arms weaken. She was losing strength as he seemed to gain it. His mouth released her and she sat up, reaching back, holding on to his thighs for balance. With her hips continuing the surge, and his arched up to meet each thrust, she looked into his eyes. Could he see the love that burned in the depths of her eyes?

Then all thoughts scattered as the swell of pleasure peaked and her climax came in a blinding rage. It burst forth, exploding into madness. He came as well, tensing then bucking wildly as tremors took them both with wave after wave of rapturous pleasure. Still looking into each other's eyes, he bucked his hips up again and she gasped as he hit the nub of her pleasure once more. She inched away, but not before he bucked and she moaned again.

Trembling, she reached for the key she'd placed on the bedside table. Too weak to move, she dragged herself up to release his hand. He immediately wrapped his arms around her and held tight, swaddling her with his love.

"I don't remember that in the book," he said, still catching his breath.

"It wasn't in the book, but maybe it should be. On second thought, maybe not."

"Why not?" he asked.

"Because I think my heart stopped beating," she whispered in total exhaustion, "I don't think I can do that again."

"Of course not," he said kissing the top of her head and nuzzling her even closer. "Next time it's my turn." He took her hand, brought it to his lips and kissed her wrist gently.

She slipped her hand away cautiously. "I don't know about that. That means I'd have to give up control and that's not an easy thing for me to do. Not anymore."

"Why not?" he asked.

"I learned the hard way that standing on my own and staying in control is a lot safer on the heart. I guess maybe I've had one too many disappointments in the past."

"Mia, control is only an illusion. What you gain is trust."

"Trust is even more difficult for me," she said. "It seems that the people I trust most let me down, like my ex. I gave him complete control over my life. I trusted him. I even allowed him to take control of my dad's place. That was a mistake. Never again. I trusted him and he betrayed me."

"Not every man is like him. People aren't perfect, Mia, but ultimately, we get past the hurt and see the best of the relationship and the love. For that you have to trust someone and let go of all fears and uncertainties. Can you do that?"

"That's not easy for some people. After being used and betrayed, you lose faith and trust. You protect your heart."

"But that's exactly when you need to open yourself up even more. You need to release all the betrayal and pain, then you'll see that not everybody's the same. Not everybody is going to hurt and deceive you, at least not intentionally."

"But what if you can't get past it?"

"Love will make you try harder," he said. "Do you still love Neal?"

"No, and the thing is, I'm not sure I really ever really did. Something always seemed to be missing in the relationship. It was forced and strained. It wasn't easy like—" She stopped suddenly, realizing she was about to confess that it wasn't easy like what the two of them shared.

"Like what?" he asked.

"Like some relationships," she said.

"I'm glad to hear that."

"Really?" she asked. He nodded. "So, is that what you did with your father—tried harder?"

"Yes."

"And it worked for you?"

"Eventually, I realized that I can't control my father. Nobody can. I can only control my reaction to him and what he does. Do I love him? Yes, do I like some of the things he does? No. But I've learned to live with that."

"You make it sound so easy."

"It's not. I had my family to help me."

"Do you think he'll change?"

"I don't know. What about your ex-fiancé?"

"I'm long past caring. I hear he's having second thoughts. Apparently the grass isn't always greener on the other side."

"It never is."

"Well, that's his problem, not mine."

"I'm glad he's out of your life."

"Me, too," she said sleepily. She sighed deeply then closed her eyes, imagining next time with their roles reversed and her tied to his bed, completely at his bidding. No control. She shuddered, liking the idea way too much.

Chapter 15

Dawn came too soon. Mia welcomed it out on the balcony wrapped in Stephen's arms. They'd been up all night, making love. Dressed only in one of Stephen's button-down shirts, she lay on his bare chest as he stroked her back lovingly.

"I think I like having you tied up and helpless," she confessed. "It's a power thing. It appeals to the dominatrix in me."

"You a dominatrix, black leather, spiked heels and a whip. That's an interesting visual. I think I like it." He chuckled.

She laughed, too. "Well, maybe not totally a dominatrix, but definitely the endorphin power-rush part. It's sexy to have power and control. You always hear about women drawn to powerful men. I guess that's why. It's a rush of total control."

"Actually the submissive has all the power," he said.

She sat up instantly and looked at him. "Oh, really?" she asked. "And you know this how?"

"You see and hear a lot of things patrolling Key West."

She laughed as she lay back down. "So tell me something. Why did you become a deputy sheriff? I get the fact that you worked with your father then quit. But you were working in a major company, and you could have worked anywhere, done anything. Why law enforcement?"

"The hospitality business isn't as pretty as it seems from the outside. I had offers, but I was burned out. I wanted to do something completely different. I wanted to help people, not intentionally harm them. It was my—"

Mia sat up confused. "Whoa, wait a minute. What do you mean you wanted to help people and not intentionally harm them? Are we talking about you masquerading as the Joker or Lex Luther here?" she asked.

Stephen smiled calmly. "Neither. I assure you I'm not a criminal mastermind bent on world domination," he said quickly, "at least not yet." He considered adding more, but didn't.

"Stephen, what happened with the fire was an accident."

"Was it? Your father didn't seem think so."

She didn't have a reply. Instead she went back to the original question. "So how exactly does the hotel business intentionally harm people?"

"The details of management can be drastic. You can completely alter a person's life with just a few words and a signature. When you're in a position of power like that, it can become addictive driven by ego. As vice president, I made business decisions that at times hurt others. I lost sensitivity."

"In most cases, isn't that just the nature of the business, any business? I mean that was your job, right? Sometimes you have to fire people or do whatever it takes."

"You can go too far. It's like the power rush you were talking about before. Ego and power are a scary mix. My father has that, but I didn't want it. As an officer, there's no ego, and the only power you wield is the power to help others."

"My dad and your father seemed to be the same type of man, strong-willed, stubborn and egotistical. I wonder if they could have been friends in a different scenario."

"Interesting thought."

"After all that you still didn't answer why you became a deputy sheriff and not a lawyer or fireman. They help people, too."

"I mentioned that my grandfather is county sheriff. I admire him, not just because he's my grandfather, but for what he stands for. He's kind, generous, patient, loving and brave. I hope I can one day come close to being as honest and forthright as he is."

"You're all those things."

"Hardly," he said.

"He sounds amazing."

"He is. I can't wait until you meet him."

"I'd like that," she said. "He's your mother's father, right?" He nodded. "And what about your grand-mother?"

"They've been married over sixty years and they're still so deeply in love. He cherishes her. It's amazing to see them together. My grandfather tells this story that he met my grandmother on a Sunday and married her on Friday."

"Is that true?"

"Yep, it's true."

"I guess when it's love and it's right, time doesn't always matter. Okay, tell me more about your mother."

"She's a great lady. She lives in Marathon and runs a huge day-care facility. After her modeling career she was a grade-school teacher. She loves children. As a matter of fact she drives me crazy, constantly trying to send me on blind dates. She's intent on getting me married so she can have a dozen grandchildren."

Mia went quiet, suddenly feeling dizzy as her stomach flipped then sank. The idea of Stephen having children with another woman was wrong. But she knew she couldn't say it. "She sounds nice," she said, already disliking the woman.

"She is, although she's been a bit annoyed with me lately."

"Why is that?"

"I refused to play her debutant dating game. I told her months ago that I'd already found the woman of my heart."

"Months ago?" Mia asked.

Before he could respond, his cell rang and he got up to answer. It was dispatch, and they needed him, he told her when he came back out onto the balcony.

Mia was standing at the rail looking out at the gray sky. She didn't turn around. "You have to go?"

Seeing Mia standing there in just his shirt made him want her all over again. His body hardened instantly. He walked up behind her, pressing close and knowing she felt his desire. "Yes," he replied. "But please stay. I want you here when I get back. We still need to talk."

She turned around, shaking her head. "I don't know if I can do that whole June Cleaver, white pearls and apron, waiting for my man to come home thing," she said teasingly. Stephen tensed and closed his eyes as if in pain. Mia touched his face gently. "Hey, are you okay? Is it your shoulder again?"

He took a deep breath then shook his head, smiling down at her as he wrapped his arm around her waist. "Woman, don't ever gave me a visual like that—you with just pearls and an apron on. I could lose my mind imagining all the ways I would make love to you."

She laughed and pushed away, but he held her too tight. His expression was serious as she looked up into his eyes.

"It's not just about the physical act of making love to you, Mia, you know that, don't you?"

She nodded slowly seeing the power of his love for her reflecting in his eyes.

"You're the one, Mia, the woman I told my mother about all those months ago."

"But how is that possible?" she asked. "We just met. I didn't know you months ago."

"Pero, mi amor, te conocía." He smiled, knowing that she understood exactly what he said.

"And how did you know me?" she asked, smirking at what she thought was an impossible admission since they'd only just met.

"I knew you because I've been waiting for you all my life. Mia, I love you." He paused then smiled. "I've loved you for a very, very long time. And now you're here with me."

She believed him. Looking into his eyes and seeing his love was all she needed. She knew in her heart that he loved her. And as impossible as it seemed, she loved him, as well. "I love you, too, Esteban, with all my heart. I can't explain it. I just know that I do. In just a few days everything in my world has turned upside down, changed, and you did that. It's like you were made for me and I just had to find you and here you are." She smiled at him, relieved to finally say the words and to hear them from his lips. "Now go to work. We'll talk later."

He grabbed her up and swung her around, laughing happily. "Are you kidding?" Stephen said. "How can I possibly just leave after waiting for so long to hear those words from you?" He stopped and let her slowly slide down the front of his body. "Mia, marry me, right now, today. I love you and I want to give you my body, my spirit, my heart, all of me. I want to cherish and love you forever and beyond even then." He fell to one knee and looked up at her. "Mia James, please marry me and be my wife."

Mia smiled shaking her head. "Stephen, this is happening way too fast. We can't get married just like that. There's so much we don't know about each other."

"We'll spend a lifetime learning. Marry me."

"This is crazy. I can't believe it," she said breathlessly, as her heart pounded in her chest. Every nerve ending was tingling and her stomach was doing somersaults. "Stephen, stand up." When he did, she looked up into his eyes.

"Mia, marry me, please."

"Stephen, I do love you, but what if this is just the hurricane or just the excitement of everything going on?"

He shook his head. "It's not. Mia, I've waited to be with you all my life. This isn't the hurricane. This is for real. My grandfather once told me that when I found the one woman for me I'd know it in my heart. Mia, you are the only woman for me. I knew it even before we spoke. I know it here," he said, taking her hand and holding it to his heart. "Marry me, please."

"I need time. I'll go to Dad's house, pick up some clothes and meet you back here later."

"No, don't leave. Wait for me here, and we'll go together."

"What if you're gone all day? I don't have anything else to wear. I can't keep wearing your shirts."

"You don't need clothes," he said huskily, as he began unbuttoning the loose top. Five buttons later he opened the shirt and gazed admiringly at her naked body. He was instantly hard.

"We don't have time for this, Deputy Sheriff Morales. You need to get to work to save the masses."

"We have all the time in the world. I'm on cruise control," he said.

"But what about breakfast? Aren't you hungry? Don't you want something to eat before you go?"

"Good idea," he said, then leaning down to lick her nipples into hardened pebbles. She gasped as he suckled her breast. She grabbed his head and held it in place, feeling the pull of his mouth and the tickle of his tongue enticing her. He, and his talented tongue, knew exactly what to do to get her wet. And she was suddenly so very, very wet.

He continued licking, kissing and sucking each breast then slowly he knelt down like before. But this time he lifted her leg over onto his shoulder. She leaned back against the rail, her arms wide, her neck stretched and her head back. As his tongue entered, her knees wobbled, weakened by his erotic intrusion. He grabbed her buttocks and pulled her closer. He found her nub and took it into his mouth. He feasted lavishly. She gasped and trembled, shaking as he suckled her to near explosion. She wanted to make it last but she couldn't stop herself. She screamed into the gray morning sky.

"I guess I was hungry after all," he said when he stood up.

Still breathing hard, she pulled the drawstring at the waistband of his sweatpants releasing them to puddle at his bare feet. He was free and ready to love her. She ran her nails down the length of his chest, feeling the hardness of his abs. She spread delicate kisses over him and around each nipple. She heard him gasp then hold his breath and knew he'd allow her to play with him as long as she desired. But she didn't want to play long. She wanted him again, this time full, thick and inside her.

While still kissing him, she reached down to grasp him. She held him tight, feeling the engorged hunger in her hand. He throbbed and pulsated as short silky curls slipped repeatedly through her fingers. He was hard and she was ready.

"Mia," he moaned, his voice deep, slow and husky. He was holding control by the thinnest thread of sanity and she wanted him to release it in her now.

She grabbed for the open shirt pocket and pulled out a condom. "I think I know us well enough to know that we need a few of these little packets every few minutes," she said when she saw him smile. She fit the condom over him, rolling it out with exaggerated slowness.

"Mia."

"Are you ready for me?" she whispered. "'Cause I'm ready for you."

That was all he needed to hear. His restraint vanished. Instantly he picked her up, holding her in a viselike grip, and laid her on her back on the chaise with him over her.

This was different, Mia thought, and she liked it. He was on top. She shivered, excited by the prospect of his power over her and in turn, her power over him.

He touched her, gently squeezing her breasts as his thumbs tickled and tantalized her already hard nipples. She arched up. "Stephen, now. Come inside me now." Either he didn't hear her or he ignored her, because he continued touching and teasing her to madness. He reached down between her legs, feeling her wetness, knowing she was ready for him again. She shuddered and called out to him, but her words were drowned out as his mouth covered hers. His kiss was hard and possessive. His tongue met hers in a frantic dance. Tremors and shockwaves began surging through her. His hands, his mouth, his tongue, his hips, all worked in unison to drive her insane with rapture.

She closed her eyes tight and writhed beneath him aching for him to be inside of her. As the intensity of passion increased, she gripped his hips in anticipation. Then she felt him. She lifted her hips to meet him and in a blinding instant he was deep inside of her. She screamed, digging her nails into his skin, holding on to him as the power of his first surge took her breath away.

He released then returned, filling her again, repeating his quick, fierce actions. He was strong and powerful and their lovemaking matched the intensity of their passion. Her heart pounded wildly as he entered her and withdrew. The swell of rapture increased, building higher and pulling tighter, threatening to explode at any second. But it didn't. They each held on, giving more, getting more.

He surged into her and she met him, thrust for thrust, welcoming him again and again. They surged higher and higher until finally she opened her eyes and looked into his. They watched as it came for them. Quick and fierce, the power of their explosion caused them both to shudder. Her legs, wrapped tightly around him, shook uncontrollably and he panted, gasping tiny breaths of air. It was magical and Mia wished her climax would never end.

Later they lay in the exact same position as earlier that morning. Mia was completely content. "You need to go," she whispered, raining tiny kisses over his chest.

"I need to stay." But he sighed heavily, knowing he was obligated elsewhere. "But you're right, I do have to leave soon."

She sat up and looked back at him still reclining on the chaise. She smiled. "You know, what you said before was right. It was kinda nice to relinquish control."

"Kinda nice, is that all?" he teased, pulling her down, lifting her leg over his body and rubbing her buttocks while pressing her close. He dipped his head to capture her breast to start their lovemaking all over again.

She laughed and moved away. "No, no, it was more than kinda nice. It was awesome."

He paused. "Okay, I guess that's a little better. But how about if we go for mind-blowing when I get back?"

She giggled as he licked her nipple. "Okay, you've got a deal. I'll meet you back here and we'll go for mind-blowingly awesome."

"No, stay here and wait for me," he urged.

"I'll think about it," she said, knowing that she'd leave just after he did. She did have pearls and her father more than likely still had the sheer apron she'd loved to wear when she'd cooked for him years ago. The idea of surprising Stephen by dressing in his fantasy when he came home was too tempting to resist.

Chapter 16

"Hey, guys, sorry I didn't call back earlier." Mia had arrived at her father's house and finally returned her stepsisters' calls. "I forgot to take my phone and since the hurricane, the signal's been going in and out anyway. Okay, let me tell you about the house and then y'all are never gonna believe what happened this morning. I still can't believe it. And then what we did in public, no less. Although in truth, no one was around except a few sea gulls, and I don't think that really counts. But before that—"

"Mia, wait. You're rambling," Janelle said.

"I know, this phone is crazy and it might go out. I can barely hear you as it is, so I'm talking fast before the signal goes. Anyway, I found out the house is basically already sold. I don't know what I can do about that yet, but I have a plan that I hope will work. I just need to get the woman in the clerk's office to give me the buyer's name. Maybe I can make a deal with them instead of the bank."

"Mia, let us give you the money. It'll be a belated birthday gift," Nya said.

Mia smiled happily thinking about their last birthday gifts to her—the book and props from Nya, and the dress and white loungewear from Janelle. Both had come in handy recently. "Thanks, guys, but no, I want to do this on my own. I have good credit and my condo is paid for. I should be able to get another mortgage on Dad's place."

"Mia, if you won't take the money as a gift then we'll call it an investment. The house will be our girls' getaway in Key West," Nya said.

"Nya, don't you already have a girls' get away on Paradise Island?"

"You can never have too many getaways," Nya said.

"I appreciate the offer, but I need to do this by myself. So what's with the dozen phone calls yesterday?"

"Tell her," Janelle said.

"Tell me what?" Mia asked.

"I did a more thorough search on that cop guy, Esteban Morales."

"Good grief, he's an axe murderer," Mia joked.

"No, Mia. Do you know who his father is?" Janelle asked.

"Yes, Carlos Morales. Stephen told me yesterday. My dad did some articles on him and his company. Dad ripped him apart pretty good."

"There's more. Carlos Morales is the owner and CEO of Morales Hotel Development. Esteban Morales is COO and vice president. It's the company that four years ago went after your father."

"No, it's other way around. Dad went after them. I read the articles he wrote. They must have been furious."

"Oh, they were furious, all right," Nya quipped sarcastically.

"What do you mean?" Mia asked. Janelle laid it out to her, telling her exactly what had happened after her father wrote the articles she read. "But there must be some mistake," Mia said, confused. "Stephen said that the articles were true. He agreed with my dad. That's why he quit the company. That's how Dad and Stephen became friends."

"Friends? Are you sure about that?" Nya asked. "According to all this I don't see how they could have been friends. You always said that your dad could hold on to a grudge for years, right?" Mia didn't respond.

"Well, I don't know how that played out, Mia, but according to everything here, Stephen and Carlos went after your father and damn near destroyed him. They trashed his career and made him disreputable in the business. That's why he stopped writing. You always blamed yourself thinking it was because of the argument you had. It wasn't."

"See," Nya said, "it had nothing to do with you or the argument about Neal."

"That's right. It looks like he was right in the middle of all this when you and he argued. He didn't quit writing because of you. He quit because of the Morales family," Janelle added.

Mia didn't answer. She was going over everything Stephen had ever said about her father. "This can't be right. If he helped ruin my father's reputation, why would Dad befriend him? It makes no sense."

"I agree. It doesn't," Nya said.

"Are you sure they were really friends?" Janelle asked.

Mia didn't answer. Janelle was right. It didn't make sense for them to become friendly as if nothing had happened. Her father wasn't that forgiving.

"Wait a minute," Janelle said, interrupting her thoughts. "What do you mean he quit? He didn't quit the business."

"Yes he did. He told me he did. That's why he's a deputy sheriff. He quit the company."

"He didn't quit, Mia," Nya said slowly, "not according to papers filed with the state board this year. It's a privately owned company without a board of directors, so there's no annual report per se, but all public records still have Stephen Morales on the payroll as vice president and COO."

"How is that possible. He's a cop with a gun and uniform and everything."

"I don't know," Nya said, "but it says in the file that both he and his dad paid some serious fines and penalties after everything happened. And by serious, I mean six-figure serious. Your dad cost them a ton of money, both businesswise and personally."

"No, it can't be. Why would he lie like that? Why would he do this to me? Why would he tell me that he…" She paused.

"Revenge maybe," Janelle suggested.

"Well, it's a good thing you didn't really continue with him. Can you imagine what he'd have up his sleeve to get back at Leo still? I wouldn't be surprised if he tried to seduce the house from under you," Nya said.

"What do you mean?" Mia asked.

"He could distract you while he takes away the last thing that belonged to your father and levels it. You said that the property was worth a lot, so wouldn't that be the ultimate revenge? Taking Leo's house and selling it would recoup some of what he paid out in fines. In the end it would be like your dad did all this for nothing."

Mia didn't reply. She was too stunned.

"I don't know about all that," Janelle said, "but I am glad you didn't keep dealing with him. He sounds too much like his father to be trusted."

"Mia, listen, the weather reports say that the hurricane is still hovering in the area, but Janelle and I are talking about flying down today. I'll talk to my friend and set it up," Nya said.

"No, don't, please. This is already such a mess. Stay there. I have to do this. I'm staying for as long as it takes."

"Do you hear yourself?" Nya asked. "You're actually talking about giving up a vacation on Paradise Island to sit in some county office begging for a reprieve."

"That's not the point. It was my dad's house and he left it to me." She looked around her childhood bedroom. It was exactly as she remembered. "It's the only thing I have of him. I can't just let it go like that. I can't walk away, not after how I left it with him."

"Mia, that's just your guilt talking. Your dad knew how much you loved him. Believe me, no silly argument could change that. Let go of the past and forgive yourself. I know he did," Janelle said.

Janelle was right. Mia did feel guilty. She'd turned her back on her father when he'd needed her most. Now it was too late to ask for forgiveness, but she could save the one thing he cared about—his beach house.

"Mia, you should leave," Nya insisted. "I mean, we understand why you're doing this, but it's a hurricane for heaven's sake. Somehow I doubt your dad would want you staying in a hurricane just to save his house."

"I have to do this," she said quietly.

"Mia, we're sorry," Janelle said. "We didn't know how to tell you, but we knew we had to."

"I know, guys. You know I'm not angry with you. I'm mad at myself for being gullible again. I guess I didn't learn anything after the Neal fiasco. Looks like I can add the Esteban fiasco to the list."

"None of this is your fault. You know that, right?" Nya asked.

"Right," Janelle added, "so don't even think that."

"You do what you have to do," Nya added, "and we'll wait to hear from you."

"Thanks, guys. I just need to tie up a few loose ends here and then I'll head directly to Paradise Island."

"We'll meet you there," Nya said.

"I thought you couldn't get away?" Mia asked.

"Change of plans," Janelle said. "We're coming."

"If you don't mind, I think I want to be by myself for a while. I need to think."

"Fine, we'll give you a few days, but then we're coming."

Nya concurred with Janelle and then added, "Mia, you know we—"

"I know," Mia interrupted. "I love you guys, too. And don't worry, I'll be fine."

Janelle and Nya continued talking, but Mia had no idea what they were saying. Her head spun in a million different directions. Everything she thought she knew was wrong. Did Stephen lie to her? And why? To hurt her like he did her father? She felt sick and dizzy all at the same time. She tossed the apron and pearls she still held in her hand across the room. "I gotta go."

"Wait, what about what you were going to tell us about this morning?" Nya said quickly.

"Never mind." Mia hung up, so furious she was shaking.

"I did it," Stephen said happily, as soon as Terrence picked up the phone at the radio station.

"Did what?" Terrence asked, instantly recognizing his friend's voice.

"I'm following your lead, man. I asked Mia to marry me."

"Hey, congratulations. That's great news."

"Thanks, although I'm not popping champagne corks just yet. I'm still waiting for an answer."

"So she's okay with everything that went down between you and Leo?" Terrence asked. He was in the middle of a play list and had time to talk.

"I didn't tell her everything yet."

"What exactly *did* you tell her?"

"I gave her the file and she read the first few articles. I'll tell her the rest this evening."

"Living kind of dangerously, aren't you?"

"She loves me. That's all that matters." Stephen couldn't keep the smile from his voice.

"Yo, man, the love thing is awesome, I totally agree, but I ain't gonna lie to you, you know there's a good chance that she's going to see this differently after everything comes out."

"Yeah, I know, but I gotta believe Leo knew what he was talking about." In fact, he was banking on it.

"I hope you're right."

"I hope so, too. All right, I gotta go. Talk to you later."

Stephen hung up then stood at the Port of Key West waiting for the last few cruise-ship passengers to disembark. The massive ship had arrived three hours earlier, but it was taking a while for the remaining passengers to leave. Apparently some passengers didn't particularly like the idea of staying in Key West to ride out Hurricane Ana's pending return. Usually the wait didn't bother him. But not today. Today all he could think about was returning to his home and finding Mia waiting there for him.

"I love you, too." The words had echoed in his thoughts all morning, making him feel as if he was walking on air. Hearing those four little words had changed everything for him. Mia was his and all he had to do now was finish telling her the truth.

He walked down Duvall Street, the town center. Most of the shops and restaurants were closed and boarded tight, a far cry from the usual gaiety and laid-back environment. Lively entertainment was the area's specialty and most visitors thrived on the adult amusements. On any given day the place was usually packed with cruise-ship tourists and locals. Of the three main docks at port, he preferred Mallory Square. It was far more interesting than either Pier B, a private dock, or the Navy Mole.

Stephen stared out at the horizon. The day had gotten increasingly gray and ominous. It was as if the universe was telling him something. The smile plastered on his face all morning had slowly dissipated. He tried to hold on to the one thing that kept him going—she loved him. She said it. But he knew he was dancing on a tightrope and any minute his world could crash down on him.

He looked out across the water. The sea was choppy and the clouds hung heavy and threatening. Meteorologists and newscasters were warning now that Hurricane Ana might return. The unsteady system had been churning in the Gulf's warm water gaining strength and power. But for right now, it was far enough away to do no immediate harm to the Keys.

He turned, drawn to the sounds of laughter as finally the passengers began to disembark. He walked back over to the ship's gangplank and stood with a ship officer to offer comments and answer questions about the port. He was afraid he failed miserably to match his usual enthusiasm.

His assignment was easily a no-brainer and just what he needed after last night and this morning. He strolled the full length of the moored ship, bow to stern, to make sure all the passengers had gotten off. When he returned to the dock he ran into his friend Lucas. Apparently his fiancée hadn't come down, but had sent someone in her stead. The beautiful woman beside him whom Lucas introduced as Doreen. Surprisingly Lucas didn't seem to mind. As a matter of fact, he seemed happier than he'd been in a long time, and the two of them strolled the pier, leaving Stephen to his assignment.

For the remainder of the afternoon Stephen did his job supporting the local police. But did so in complete mental absence. He went through the motions, but that was all. His thoughts were miles away with Mia. He'd called his home several times, and her cell, but she hadn't picked up.

"I love you, too." Her words repeated in his head but his heart was troubled. He knew instinctively something was wrong. She'd either read the rest of the file or she'd somehow found out the rest of the story on her own. Either way, it was not how he wanted her to know the truth. He knew he should have told her, that way he could be there and explain. His feeble attempt to come clean earlier was pathetic. He had the perfect opportunity last night, but when she'd stripped, he'd lost all senses. Now his time was up and taking the call from dispatch only delayed telling the truth. How could he just walk out and not finish what he started? He called her cell again, and she picked up instantly. "Mia, it's—"

She cut him off right away. "Why didn't you tell me the whole story last night?"

Stephen stood silent. He knew she'd figure it out eventually, he'd just hoped it wouldn't be like this. "Leo wrote the article about my father. The company was—"

"And why didn't you tell me who you were in the beginning?"

"It didn't matter."

"It didn't matter? Are you joking? You and your father harassed my father for years. You ruined him."

"That's not quite how it happened, Mia."

"That's exactly how it happened, Esteban. My father wrote the article and your father went after him. Tell me, did my father even know who you really were?" When he didn't respond, she pressed on. "He didn't, did he? You tricked him, didn't you? You lied and betrayed him just like you did me. I guess that's the ultimate revenge on him."

"Mia, it wasn't like that. Leo knew me. We were friends."

"Did he know your father, too? Were they friends also?"

"My father has nothing to do with this."

"He has everything to do with this. He isn't some kind of martyred hero, and my father wasn't an over-zealous hack. My dad was a good man. He was honest and truthful. If he wrote that your father cheated and lied, then he did. You and your—" She paused to take a deep breath and collect herself. "Four years ago you and your father deliberately ruined a good man's reputation just because he wrote the truth."

"Mia," Stephen said, knowing there was nothing he could say to explain what actually happened. "Leo wasn't perfect, he had flaws. I know this isn't easy for you to hear, but he did."

"I'm done listening, Stephen. You really had me fooled. All that charm and charisma. I actually fell for it."

"Mia, stop, just listen to me," he said calmly, hoping she'd calm down, too.

"Listen to what? Is this considered police brutality?"

"No, this is considered love."

"Oh, please, don't you dare talk to me about love. You don't have the first clue what love is. Love isn't betrayal and lies and deceit. Love isn't stealing some-one's home and hiding behind a badge, and love isn't…you."

"Please, Mia, just listen to what I have to say. If you still want to walk away, then fine."

"There's nothing you can tell me that I haven't already figured out."

"How about the truth?" he asked. "You're right, there's nothing I can tell you. But you are your father's daughter, so do him one last justice. Find out the truth for yourself."

"I already know that truth."

"You're not even close."

She hung up. Her first thought was to find Stephen and rip his heart out. But then she realized that he probably didn't even have one. Liars and betrayers didn't, or if they did it was either frozen solid or solid stone. Either way she was through.

Stephen was just like Neal. They'd do anything and say anything to get what they wanted. They both used her and manipulated the truth to their advantage. She knew Neal's reasoning. He was a spineless mama's boy with visions of grandeur. Stephen's reasoning was still a mystery. But then Janelle was probably right. Perhaps he wanted the ultimate revenge and she gave it to him. She'd fallen in love and he'd crushed her.

Mia stormed into her bedroom and began packing. She slammed her clothes into the open suitcase. This was over. She'd lost the house and she'd lost her heart. There was nothing left for her here. She intended to get as far away from Key West as possible.

As she packed, Stephen's words echoed in her mind over and over again. *"You are your father's daughter, so do him one last justice. Find out the truth for yourself."* She didn't have to find out the truth. She knew it and he confessed it. The only question was why.

Then she thought about the file Stephen had insisted she read the night before. She'd only read the first few articles. They'd shed a light of some of what her sisters said, so she wondered what else might be inside. She knew there had to be more to the story. As her father always said, knowledge was ninety-nine percent perceptions. If you want to find information, you have to research. But if you want to find the truth, you have to get dirty and dig for it.

Fine, she was ready for the truth.

Chapter 17

Mia went back to Stephen's house and found the file still where she tossed it the night before. She sat, opened it, flipped past the first three articles and began reading the rest of the hefty file.

The more she read the more questions she had and the harder it was to wade through the convoluted mess of charges, countercharges and childish finger-pointing. None of this made sense. What was a simple exposé turned into a major conflict. In newspaper lingo, blood had been drawn and the battle between her father and Carlos Morales and his company had begun.

Tirades on both sides were extreme and apparently the ethical damages to careers were irreversible. The ensuing rampage resulted in libel and defamation lawsuits from both sides. There were accusations of ethical corruption, allegations of perjury, bribery, corruption and fraud. But the last and final blow was leveled by Stephen. It was disastrous and ultimately career-ending, resulting in her father being quietly discharged from his publisher, and thanks to Stephen, no other publication would touch him.

Mia closed the file, stunned by what she'd read. She had no idea any of this had gone on. Her father had told her that *he'd* decided to leave his job. She'd never quite accepted his reason of wanting a quieter lifestyle. He was too addicted to print and investigative research. Even then she'd suspected there was more. Apparently she'd been right.

She left Stephen's house, but instead of going back to her father's home, she headed into town. Her father had a good friend on the local newspaper staff and she hoped he could tell her more. She went to the newspaper office, but unfortunately her dad's friend was out covering a story. She hung around for a bit, and then decided to dig into some of the old newspaper files herself.

She inquired about past issues and was directed to the archive section. She spent the next two hours reading everything pertaining to the legal battle. There were dozens of articles, by other reporters, about the Morales family, more particularly Carlos Morales. By all accounts he wasn't the kind of man with whom you made enemies. Her father had done exactly that. Carlos had a serious reputation in and out of the business for being tyrannical, heartless and vindictive. He was stubborn and pigheaded, just like her father. No wonder they didn't get along.

Her father continued writing his exposés on Carlos Morales and Morales fired back. The ongoing attacks waged back and forth for months. With the added pressure he sparked with his articles, city planners, the building commission and construction regulators had been scheduled to inspect the hotel. But one week before the inspection the hotel—in mid-construction—conveniently burned down. The final report stated accidental, but her father didn't buy it. He accused the department of corruption and accepting bribes.

Attacks on both sides continued, the final blow pushing Leo into permanent retirement and damaging the Morales name and reputation.

Mia was stunned. She couldn't believe what she was reading. The more she learned, the less she wanted to. By all accounts it looked as if the Morales family, with their extended resources and influence, pushed her father out of the business and systematically ruined his career.

"Mia."

Mia looked up from her stack of old newspapers and files, to see Helen from the clerk's office standing at the counter beside her. "I thought that was you. What a coincidence seeing you here. I was just dropping off your papers for the public announcement. I just now found out from the bank that the bid for your house was accepted. Congratulations."

Mia was devastated, but she tried not to show it. She knew saving the house was a long shot at best. "Thanks, Helen. Did you ever find out who bid on it?"

"Yes, but it's of course confidential."

"I see. Well, thanks for all your help," Mia said.

"Well, I'm sure it won't do any harm to tell you now. Besides you'll have to sign some papers in the morning and the buyer will be there. As a matter of fact I'm sure you'll even be happy that the property will be in such

good hands." She looked around secretively and then
leaned in closer to Mia. "Stephen Morales put in the
highest bid. He used considerable pull to win this par-
ticular bid. He paid a lot more than anticipated. I'm
sure you can expect a nice sum after all the debts are
paid."

Mia tried her best not to scream. This was impossible. How was this real? Stephen, the man she fallen
for, the man she'd been with for the last three days, had
stolen her house from under her and never said a word.
She looked at him and his father smiling in one of the
newspaper photos in front of her. Suddenly it all made
sense.

Stephen's cell rang. Hoping it was Mia, he checked
the caller ID. It wasn't her. He answered with a barked-
out, "Yeah."

"Don't 'yeah' me, what's going on?"

"Not now, Gnat, I'm busy. I'm on duty."

"I know you're on duty. If you weren't you'd be here
seeing what I'm seeing."

Stephen shook his head and sighed heavily. At times
Natalia had a way of cutting straight to the point of any
conversation. Then other times she was completely
cryptic. This was one of those times. "What are you
talking about?"

"I'm in town. Mia's here and she looks pissed."

"Why is Mia there?" he asked. Even so, he was
almost afraid to hear the answer.

"I have no idea. I saw her coming out of the newspaper office. The expression on her face was murder-
ous. She knows, doesn't she? You told her and she's
pissed."

"One expression told you all that?" he asked.

"Yes. It wasn't the expression so much as her blank stare. It was unmistakable. It looked like she'd been sucker punched, knocked down and just got up looking for blood. Believe me, I know the look. I've had it a few times myself."

He sighed again. "You're right that she knows, but I didn't tell her." He whispered, "I tried to, but I couldn't."

"What are you going to do?"

"I don't really know. She's angry, so I'm giving her some time, some space. I told her to find the truth for herself."

"One more thing, I ran into Helen Parker from the county office. She mentioned that she ran into Mia at the newspaper office a few hours ago when she was posting the foreclosure listings. Apparently Mia wanted the name of the new owner of her father's property to see if she could make a deal."

Stephen went still. "Don't tell me she told her."

"She would have found out anyway."

Stephen ran a hand over his face as he began to pace. "But now it looks like I did all this on purpose, for spite or even revenge. I didn't want her find out about the house being auctioned to me."

"That option, dear cousin, is no longer on the table. The question now is what are you going to do about it?"

"I asked Mia to marry me this morning."

"Did she accept?"

"We were supposed to talk about it this evening."

"I'd say that's probably off the table, as well."

He looked around. "I'm just about done, so I'll check out from here."

"Yeah, you do that. I'll see you later."

Stephen closed his cell and walked away. It was time to confront his past and hopefully his future.

A half hour later, after a brief stop at his home, Stephen knocked on Leo James's door. He got no answer. Knowing Mia was there, he turned the knob and walked in. The first thing he saw were her suitcases sitting by the front door.

Chapter 18

After leaving town, Mia spent the rest of the afternoon in the attic going through her father's boxes. They had now become her main source of information on his life. As Stephen had said before, her father kept everything—every article he'd ever written, every letter he'd ever received. She plowed through the boxes trying to keep his ordered system in place while searching for anything related to Stephen and his father. What she found was far different than she expected. Her father, the perfect man she thought she knew, was a man she didn't know at all.

By reading his journals, she found her father's Pulitzer Prize–winning career had ended with alcoholism, plagiarism and perjury. He'd changed and he had destroyed everything around him. The scandals had humiliated and broken him in the end and he'd lost everything, including her.

By all accounts, it wasn't until a year before his death that he came to terms with his troubles. That was also around the time he had become friends with Stephen. The change in him and his writing was evident. But by that time she herself was still too angry, stubborn and wrapped up in her life. In the end she'd missed the best part of her father and would always regret that loss.

The last journal stated that medical and legal expenses had completely wiped him out. He was broke. He had a second mortgage on the house and a lien and was basically living day-to-day. He was too proud and stubborn to say anything except to his friend Stephen, who often helped him out, both financially and emotionally. Stunned, she read the paragraph again seeing in her father's own writing that he considered Stephen a friend. She closed the last journal and just stared out the window.

Mia heard knocking at the front door. She knew it was Stephen. She didn't answer, knowing that he'd let himself in and find her. Moments later she looked up to see him standing in the doorway. He held an envelope in his hand but she didn't speak. She was way past anger and retribution. She just looked at him blankly.

"Mia," he began, then paused and looked around seeing open boxes and Leo's journals on the desk. "Did you find what you needed?" he questioned. She nodded once. "And now you're leaving?"

"What are you doing here?"

"We need to talk."

"I don't think so."

"You know just about everything, Mia, but—"

"Just about?" she interrupted.

"There are things not in the articles and journals that you don't know. The truth—"

"The truth is that you and your father went after everything my dad had. The truth is he was sick and you didn't care. It wasn't enough that you got him fired and banned from writing. No, you sued him for libel then took everything he had. You even put a lien on this house. Then after he died I guess you came after me."

"Mia, you know that's not how it happened. I know it looks that way, but believe me—"

She laughed. "Are you joking? Believe you? So wait, are you going to stand there and tell me now that everything is a lie? You didn't have anything to do with any of this?" she asked, holding up the newspapers announcing his father's retirement.

"No."

"Good, at least you manned up about that."

"I did exactly what the articles say I did. I went after Leo because I thought he libeled my father and my family. I believed that he lied in his article and I did everything in my power to bring him down. But what the articles don't say is that—" He stopped and looked away.

"Is that what?"

He just stood there shaking his head knowing that anything he said would be wrong. He'd never have Mia if he told her the real truth. Her father wasn't the hero, the perfect man she always made him out to be. She needed to learn it on her own. "I'm sorry about everything."

"Sorry?" she said calmly. "You and your father destroy people and ruin lives and all you can say is that you're sorry? So tell me, did you get a big laugh out of me telling you that I loved you this morning? I bet that was the topper on the humiliation meter. It added the cherry to your already perfect day. You got his house and you got his daughter. You must be feeling pretty good right about now."

"I didn't tell you everything because I didn't want to scare you away."

"Scare me away from what?"

"From loving me as much as you do."

She opened her mouth, but she had no rebuttal. He knew her too well. The truth was, she did love him.

"And," Stephen added, "as much as I love you."

"Oh, please, do you really expect me to believe that?"

"It's true and you know it. I love you."

"To quote a famous lady, 'What's love got to do with it?'"

"Everything."

"I can't do this."

"Yes, you can. This isn't about Leo and my father and all that other stuff anymore. It's about us, now, you and me together. I love you, Mia. I don't know how to stop feeling what I feel and I know I wouldn't even if I could. You're angry, I get it. You have every right to be. But know that nothing will ever change my feelings for you."

Mia looked at him seeing that he was telling the truth, but she refused to weaken, not now. Him saying that he loved her didn't matter. He'd betrayed her father and her, that's what mattered. "Leave."

"Mia, please," he began again as he reached out to her.

"Just go, Stephen. I can't do this anymore," she said calmly.

He nodded slowly then placed a manila envelope on the desk. He backed up then slowly turned to the door.

"Wait, I have one question," she said as he stood

with his back to her. "How could you have possibly been friends? Nothing here says why. Didn't he know who you were and what you did to him?"

"He knew."

She waited for more, but he didn't continue. "That's all you have to say—'he knew'? No, it's not that easy this time, Stephen. I know my father, he held a grudge forever. He and my mom had been divorced for years and he still held a grudge. There's no way he just up and forgave you for what you did to him."

"He knew," Stephen said quietly then walked out.

Mia stood there a moment, not sure why she was so angry with Stephen. In the end he'd stepped up to do what she refused to. He saved her father and became his friend. She picked up her cell and dialed.

Mia told her stepsisters everything that had happened since they'd spoken that morning—the file at Stephen's house, the archived articles at the newspaper office, and the conversation with Helen Parker. The information was more damning than she realized. She ended with her last conversation with Stephen.

"And that's all he said, just that 'he knew'?" Janelle questioned her.

"What else could he say? He got caught," Mia replied. "How could I have been so stupid? I fell for a pack of lies again."

"Not necessarily," Janelle said.

"I agree," Nya echoed. "So what exactly did the articles say about Stephen?"

"Basically that he quit his father's business shortly afterward and came to work as a sheriff down here with his grandfather."

"So you think maybe he didn't have a whole lot to

do with what happened with your dad? That's probably why he and Leo were friends."

"No, he was definitely there at the time. Everything I read said that both he and his father spearheaded the attack. Somehow they found out that my father was accused of false reporting and plagiarism in one of his articles to get better press. The man he wrote about, a guy named Kellerman, eventually killed himself. Nothing was ever proven about my father. But if indeed he wrote lies, it was not only unethical, but also reprehensible and culpable. A man died and that was something he had to live with."

"So maybe the Moraleses were protecting themselves. I mean if you're saying it's true that your dad lied in one of his articles, maybe he lied about Stephen's company, too, and they were defending themselves."

"They both lied—my dad and Carlos Morales. They were both wrong. This is so crazy," Mia said. "It just doesn't make any sense. Why would my dad and Stephen become friends?"

"Because Leo forgave him," Janelle said.

"Believe me, Janelle, Leo James never forgave anybody for anything."

"Maybe it was guilt," Nya said. "Maybe he felt guilty about what he wrote."

"And maybe Stephen really does love you," Janelle added changing the subject. "It sure sounds like it to me."

"To me, too," Nya concurred. "And you love him."

"How can I possibly love the man who ruined my father's career?"

"You can and you do, face it."

Nya agreed with Janelle. "Of course you can. So he's not perfect, so he had drama with your dad. So what? Your dad let it go, and you can, too, especially since you love him. And FYI, girl, your father ruined his career, not Stephen."

"Mia, don't you think people change?" Janelle asked.

"I really don't know," she said.

"Yes you do. Your dad changed, Stephen changed. Can you?"

"So what's in the envelope he gave you?" Nya asked.

"I don't know," Mia said passively.

"Open it," Janelle insisted.

"Why? There's nothing he can possibly say, do or give me that would change what happened. He helped ruin my father and he lied to me. I can't just let that go. Love or not, I'm done."

"You don't know that, Mia. Finish this the right way. You know you're not going to be satisfied with anything less."

"Wait a minute. Earlier today you were both delighted that I didn't have anything to do with him. Now, after I tell you what happened between us and then everything I found out, you're all for me giving him a chance."

"That's not what we're saying," Janelle said. "Mia, you know in your heart that you need to know the rest of the story. The fact that you're in love with the man is beside the point. There are still too many questions left unanswered. And maybe you're willing to just walk away right now because you're mad, but one day you're gonna want the answers and you know it. There's only one real way you're gonna get those answers. That's from your dad. Since that's impossible, Stephen's your next best source."

"A source that has his own agenda," Mia said.

"Janelle's right, Mia," Nya added. "You know you can't stand not knowing the whole truth about something. Remember how you dug and dug until you found out everything about Neal? You weren't satisfied until it was over. Then you moved on."

"Yeah, and look want I moved on to, falling in love again."

"Open the package and see what's inside."

"Fine." Mia reached over, grabbed the envelope and opened it. "Letters," she said simply after peeking inside.

"To whom, from whom?" Nya asked.

"I don't know and I don't care," Mia said, tossing the package back down on the desk.

"Aren't you even curious?" Nya asked.

"Why would I be?"

"You just said that your father's journals were enlightening. Maybe Stephen's letters are, too. You'll never know until you read them," Nya said. "Remember, they were friends."

"Close friends," Janelle corrected.

"I still don't get it. How could Dad be friends with the man who ruined his career, the only thing he ever really loved? Writing was his life and Stephen took that away."

"Maybe the only way you're going to find out is to read Stephen's letters."

She grabbed the envelope again and pulled out the stack of about two dozen letters. They were all addressed to her from her father. They were stamped and mailed to her, in care of Stephen. She gasped. "Oh my God," she whispered.

"What is it?" both Nya and Janelle asked.

"Um, the letters aren't from Stephen. They're addressed to me from my dad in care of Esteban Morales. They were mailed to him for me almost a year ago."

"You need to read them," Nya said.

"I don't think I'm ready for this."

"You are. You're strong, you can do it. Read them and call us back," Janelle said.

"I don't know."

"Yes, you do," Nya said. "Call us right back."

Mia closed her cell and picked up the first letter. She opened it and read the date. It was the day before her father died. She quickly folded it and stuffed it back into the envelope. She began breathing hard. This was too much. There was no way she could do this, but she knew she had to if she was ever going to get beyond this.

She turned the stack over and grabbed the bottom letter. She opened it and read the date. It was written about a year ago. Calming down, she slowly began to read. When she was finished, she opened the second and then continued from there. She laughed at times and cried at other times. Each letter explained more and more about her father's relationship with Stephen and his hopes for her.

By the time she got to the last envelope she was on a roller-coaster ride of confusing emotions. She already knew the date of this letter. She slowly slid the letter out of the envelope. She unfolded it, reread the date and then got filled up all over again. This was the last letter her father wrote her. She read it then began laughing and crying all at once. When she finished she read it a few more times then folded it and put it back in the envelope and called her sisters. She summarized the letters, but actually read the last letter to them.

"Oh my God," Nya exclaimed. "It's like he was standing right next to you talking, explaining everything."

"This is so eerie. He knew Stephen was falling in love with you and he helped make it happen. He even knew that you'd fall in love with Stephen."

Mia was speechless. "What do I do with this?"

"It's like your father's last wish was for you to be happy and he knew Stephen would make you happy," Janelle said.

"This is so incredible. It's like a fairy tale," Nya added.

"It doesn't matter. He did what he did," Mia said.

"Mia, don't be blinded by your stubbornness," Janelle said. "Forgive him."

"What he did to my father—"

"What your father did to himself," Janelle corrected. "Besides, your father forgave him, he even befriended him. Why can't you? Let it go, girl, just let it go. Nya, what's that you always say?"

"Life is short, so forgive fast. Break some rules along the way and never forget to laugh at yourself."

"Yeah, that," Janelle said. "Forgive fast."

"There's one more thing that happened this morning," Mia said cautiously.

"You mean besides him rocking your world on the open balcony?" Nya said, still amused by Mia's earlier confession.

"Yeah, besides that. He proposed to me."

"What?" they both shouted.

"How you gonna leave something like that out?" Nya said.

"You talked about motives before. Girl, the man's motives are clear. He's in love and it sounds like you love him, too, don't you?"

"Yes, I do, and I don't know how to stop."

"Don't," Janelle said.

"But I just kicked him out of here."

"I wouldn't worry about that," Nya said. "Somehow I think he's sitting someplace right now waiting for you."

"I hope you're right."

Chapter 19

Terrence and Lucas stopped by. Stephen definitely wasn't in the mood to deal with his friends, but they weren't going to let him just sit and brood. The three of them sat out on the balcony talking about Hurricane Ana and its effects on all their lives. The Category One storm had hit a large portion of Florida and the Keys, but Key West was spared its worst. The hurricane still lurked a hundred miles offshore and meteorologists warned that it could return.

"You should have told her, man," Terrence said, leaning back against the rail with a cold beer in his hand. Behind him the angry Gulf churned and pushed the last remnants of Hurricane Ana out to sea.

"The time was never right," Stephen said.

"It was never going to be right. You know that," Lucas added. "Terrence has a point, hindsight and all. You should have told her everything in the beginning."

"Yeah, I know, but she would have slammed the door in my face or, better yet, thought I was insane. Besides, none of that matters, now. It's too late. She's leaving town."

"You know that for a fact?" Lucas asked.

"Her bags were packed and sitting by the door. The weather's cleared up enough and the bridges are open."

"Did you give her the letters you were holding for her?"

"Yeah." He looked at his watch. "About three hours ago. I haven't heard anything, not a word."

"Come on, man, you know women want to make a brotha wait," Terrence said jokingly. Both Stephen and Lucas smiled, but the seriousness of the conversation hung too heavy. "But seriously, you know what they say about the first hurricane winds bringing change."

"That's right. In a matter of just a few days one hurricane is changing all our lives," Lucas said. "Look at me and my fiancée, our new home is almost complete and I have no idea what's going to happen. Emma's growing more and more distant and I'm having second thoughts. She didn't come down as promised, but Doreen did." He shrugged without finishing the thought. "And look at Terrence. All he wanted to do was buy a radio station and he found the love of his life."

"And so Mia will miraculously change her mind, let go of the past, realize that she still loves me and come knocking on the door?" Stephen asked. He looked at his friends. They shrugged and nodded at the possibility. "Look, I'm happy for you both, you know that. But this is different."

"Hurricane Ana is still out there. This isn't over yet." Terrence said, raising his bottle. Lucas tapped it lightly, toasting the comment.

Stephen listened to his friends' positive comments, but in his heart he feared the worst. Lives weren't ruled by hurricane winds, and Mia had every right to be angry. He hurt her and he wasn't sure their love could go beyond the anger. He knew she loved him, but her stubbornness, like her father's, might not allow her to let it go. Leo had come around and he had hoped that Mia would, too. But she hadn't. How could he have been so wrong? How could he have misjudged everything so completely?

They went on to discuss Terrence's woman, Sherrie and Lucas's friend, Doreen. Both guys seemed to be floating on cloud nine with their new relationships. Stephen listened and laughed appropriately but his thoughts were still with Mia.

Terrence turned, seeing someone walking on the beach toward the pier. "Hey, now who would be out this late walking out there?"

Stephen moved to the rail and looked out. "Mia," Stephen whispered, recognizing her instantly. He watched as she continued walking down the length of the pier to stand at the rail.

"Looks like she's waiting for you," Terrence said. "Come on, Lucas, let's get out of here."

A few minutes later Stephen opened the back gate and walked down to the beach then to the pier. Mia stood at the rail looking out at the horizon. He walked up and stood behind her. She turned knowing he was there with her, and he saw that she'd been crying. "Mia," he began.

"No, Stephen, I need an answer."

She didn't ask a question because she knew that he already knew what she wanted to know. He nodded and looked out to sea. It was late and darkness was near.

Clouds hung heavy as he began. "Years ago I bought the property and built the house, but I didn't move in right away. I was working too hard. I obviously knew who Leo was, but not that we lived so close. He did. Later, after I left the company and became a sheriff, I arrested him. I knew who he was at the time, but he was too intoxicated to recognize me. I picked him up, or rather detained him, for drunken and disorderly conduct. All he talked about was his Mia. I didn't care at first. I just wanted to do my job and get it over with.

"Later, after he sobered up, he walked up the beach just like you just did and stood looking up at my house. I saw him and I came down. I had no idea what to expect. He wanted to know about the Kellerman information I used against him. He asked about my source. But I wouldn't tell him." He paused and looked at her.

She tipped the corner of her mouth up. "They weren't all lies, were they? He did fabricate the truth, didn't he?"

Stephen didn't answer the question. "After the articles he wrote about the company, I dug around and found out about the Kellerman scandal and how he went out of business and then killed himself." He saw Mia grimace, and he knew that hearing the truth wasn't as easy as she'd imagined it would be. "I couldn't find any legitimate proof, just hearsay and innuendo. I had leads and I followed them, but nothing panned out.

"At the time I assumed my father was innocent of the charges leveled against him in the exposé. It was my assertion that if Leo lied once, he could have done it again. Then I got an anonymous folder with everything I needed on the Kellerman article to take Leo down. I ran with it."

"And that ended his career," she said.

Stephen nodded. "I got another anonymous folder a

few days later. Inside was proof that everything in Leo's article about my father was true."

"And that ended your career," she said. "Who sent you the anonymous folders?" When Stephen shook his head, she asked, "You never found out, or you're not going to tell me?"

"Leo once told me that a good investigative reporter never revealed his source."

Mia smiled for the first time. "Thank you."

"For what?" he asked.

"For protecting your source," she said.

"You know he sent them to me, don't you?" he said. "But he didn't write it in his journals. There was nothing."

"Dad always felt guilty about Mr. Kellerman," Mia said. Then seeing Stephen's surprised expression, she nodded and half smiled. "Yeah, I knew about Kellerman. Dad didn't think I knew, but I did. I figured it out, but he never admitted it."

"It was like he wanted it to happen."

Neither one spoke for a while. They just stood quiet looking out at the sea. Then Mia turned and looked at him.

"Tell me something. Are you still with your father's company?"

"Technically my name is still connected to safeguard the business, but that's all. My father needed it to secure outside financing. The company was near bankruptcy. Fees, fines and retributions after the legal battles nearly ruined it. I agreed to keep my name attached, but one of the provisions when I left was that all operations be mandated by outside regulators of my choosing. I have a very good friend of mine taking care of that."

"So pop inspections, that kind of thing?"

He nodded. "Yes, among other things. Everything is by the book. It's costly, but it's worth it."

"One of your provisions. Are there others?"

"Yes, several dozen or so. Another one is that my company salary goes to my mother's child-care centers."

Mia smiled shaking her head. "You and children again."

"Mia," he began.

"The thing is, I wish I knew about all this before. I'm not saying I agree with any of it. The whole thing was crazy, but it's in the past. My father got beyond it. I don't know how but he did. Funny, reading his letters was exactly what I needed. I guess he knew I'd have questions."

Stephen nodded. "I had explicit orders from him to give them to you when you needed them. But if you married Neal, I was to burn them, because he felt you'd have truly moved on."

"I miss writing him. I bet between the two of us we kept the United States postal service in business. He hated phone calls. I guess I should have known something was strange when he called me that last time," she said thickly then stepped back to walk away. "I have to leave."

"Why?" he asked, taking her hand.

"In case you haven't noticed, there's not a whole lot down here for me anymore."

"That's not true. I'm here."

"Stephen, I do love you. I don't know how to stop feeling what I feel for you. This never happened to me before. How do we just be friends now?"

"I don't want to be just your friend, Mia, I can't. I want more. I want all of you. I know I hurt you and I should have told you everything up front. I was wrong."

"Before, earlier, I thought we were over, and I thought I'd be okay with it. But you know what? It's not okay."

"It's never gonna be okay. We belong together. I let you push me away earlier, but never again. If that means I have to fight for you for the rest of my life just to prove that we belong together, then I'll do it. I love you with all my heart. The only thing between us that matters is what we feel."

"How do we do this—have a long-distance relationship?"

"I'm going to quit the force here and move to Atlanta."

"No, I can't ask you to do that. I don't want you to do that. This is your home."

"If you think a long-distance relationship will be enough for us, you're wrong." He smiled. "And phone sex isn't gonna do it for either of us. Mia, I don't ever want to be parted from you again."

"You won't be. I'm moving down here."

"Really?"

She nodded. "Really. My dad wanted me to keep this place. I guess I can find someplace to live."

"I don't think that will be a problem."

"Anyway, thank you for the letters."

"I have one more thing for you. I saved it."

"What is it?"

"It's at the house. Come on."

She followed as he led the way back down the beach to his home. She waited on the balcony while he went into the house. Standing there staring out at the colorful sky, she felt complete. After everything that had happened she loved him more than ever. It was strange. With Neal, there was nothing, no feeling, no emotion.

But with Stephen everything was clear and she had no idea why or how. It was irrational, but it was real. It wasn't about forgiveness or change or right and wrong. It was about love and she did love him.

"Here it is," Stephen said behind her.

Not knowing what to expect, Mia turned. She instantly stopped breathing and her heart skipped a beat. "Stephen," she whispered, smiling and half laughing upon seeing what he held. He walked closer and placed the jar of sea glass in her shaking hands. She almost dropped it. He grabbed hold, keeping it secure in her trembling hands. "Where did you find this?" she muttered, placing the jar on the table.

"Leo gave it to me to keep for you."

Mia reached in and grabbed a handful of colorful smooth glass and then let them go, smiling happily. "My mermaid's tears, I thought he'd lost them. I can't believe it. Thank you." She reached out to him. He grabbed hold and held her tight. She snuggled close filled with a love she'd never imagined. This was her home. This was where she belonged, with Stephen, in his arms forever. "My head is spinning right now. I don't know if I'm coming or going."

"You're staying, Mia, that's all that matters. *Usted, mi amor es mi fantasía.* I've been waiting for you for so long and now you're here in my arms."

"I think we've both been waiting long enough."

"You know you still didn't answer my question from this morning. Will you marry me?"

"Yes, yes, yes."

Deliriously happy to finally get the answer he wanted, he picked her up and swung her around. They both laughed happily until he slowly released her. They stood gazing into each other's eyes. The hurricane winds blew gently as a patch of sunset cleared in the distance. It wasn't over. It was just the beginning.

Mother Nature has love on her mind…

Temperatures Rising

Book #1 in *Mother Nature Matchmaker…*

New York Times Bestselling Author

BRENDA JACKSON

Radio producer Sherrie Griffin is used to hot, stormy weather. But the chemistry between her and sports DJ Terrence Jeffries is a whole new kind of tempest. Stranded together during a Florida hurricane, they take shelter…in each other's arms.

*Mother Nature has something brewing…
and neither man nor woman stands a chance.*

*Coming the first week of May 2009,
wherever books are sold.*

KIMANI™
ROMANCE

REQUEST YOUR FREE BOOKS!

2 FREE NOVELS
PLUS 2 FREE GIFTS!

KIMANI™
ROMANCE

Love's ultimate destination!

YES! Please send me 2 FREE Kimani™ Romance novels and my 2 FREE gifts (gifts are worth about $10). After receiving them, if I don't wish to receive any more books, I can return the shipping statement marked "cancel." If I don't cancel, I will receive 4 brand-new novels every month and be billed just $4.69 per book in the U.S. or $5.24 per book in Canada. That's a savings of over 20% off the cover price. It's quite a bargain! Shipping and handling is just 50¢ per book.* I understand that accepting the 2 free books and gifts places me under no obligation to buy anything. I can always return a shipment and cancel at any time. Even if I never buy another book from Kimani Press, the two free books and gifts are mine to keep forever.

168 XDN EYQG   368 XDN EYQS

Name	(PLEASE PRINT)	

Address		Apt. #

City	State/Prov.	Zip/Postal Code

Signature (if under 18, a parent or guardian must sign)

Mail to **The Reader Service:**
IN U.S.A.: P.O. Box 1867, Buffalo, NY 14240-1867
IN CANADA: P.O. Box 609, Fort Erie, Ontario L2A 5X3

Not valid to current subscribers of Kimani Romance books.

Want to try two free books from another line?
Call 1-800-873-8635 or visit www.morefreebooks.com.

* Terms and prices subject to change without notice. Prices do not include applicable taxes. Sales tax applicable in N.Y. Canadian residents will be charged applicable provincial taxes and GST. Offer not valid in Quebec. This offer is limited to one order per household. All orders subject to approval. Credit or debit balances in a customer's account(s) may be offset by any other outstanding balance owed by or to the customer. Please allow 4 to 6 weeks for delivery. Offer available while quantities last.

Your Privacy: Kimani Press is committed to protecting your privacy. Our Privacy Policy is available online at www.eHarlequin.com or upon request from the Reader Service. From time to time we make our lists of customers available to reputable third parties who may have a product or service of interest to you. If you would prefer we not share your name and address, please check here. ☐

KROM09

NATIONAL BESTSELLING AUTHOR

ROCHELLE ALERS

INVITES YOU TO MEET THE BEST MEN...

Close friends Kyle, Duncan and Ivan have become rich,
successful co-owners of a beautiful Harlem brownstone. But
they lack the perfect women to share their lives with—until
true love transforms them into grooms-to-be....

Man of Fate
June 2009

Man of Fortune
July 2009

Man of Fantasy
August 2009

ARABESQUE®

www.kimanipress.com
www.myspace.com/kimanipress

KPRABMSP